Savannah Spectator

Blind Item

There is no lack of scandal in the Garden of Good and Evil. And it's no secret that one of Savannah's proudest families has experienced more than their share of it lately. But this latest blow to their previously unblemished reputation just may be the final nail in the coffin of Daddy's senatorial run. Just how will they survive a younger son's indictment for racketeering?

But that's not all, folks. Although previously unattached, Younger Son is about to announce his engagement to a young woman of a questionable social background. Just how the couple intends to plan their wedding with the groom behind bars remains to be seen. Now all the family needs to add is an unplanned baby and we'd have a first-rate Savannah scandal that novelists and filmmakers would love to get their hands on! I hear Hollywood just might be interested....

Dear Reader,

Welcome to another passionate month at Silhouette Desire where the menu is set with another fabulous title in our DYNASTIES: THE DANFORTHS series. Linda Conrad provides *The Laws of Passion* when Danforth heir Marc must clear his name or face the consequences. And here's a little something to whet your appetite—the second installment of Annette Broadrick's THE CRENSHAWS OF TEXAS. What's a man to do when he's *Caught in the Crossfire*— actually, when he's caught in bed with a senator's daughter? You'll have to wait and see....

Our mouthwatering MANTALK promotion continues with Maureen Child's *Lost in Sensation*. This story, entirely from the hero's point of view, will give you insight into a delectable male—what fun! Kristi Gold dishes up a tasty tidbit with *Daring the Dynamic Sheikh*, the concluding title in her series THE ROYAL WAGER. Rochelle Alers's series THE BLACKSTONES OF VIRGINIA is back with *Very Private Duty* and a hunk you can dig right into. And be sure to save room for the delightful treat that is Julie Hogan's *Business or Pleasure?*

Here's hoping that this month's Silhouette Desire selections will fulfill your craving for the best in sensual romance... and leave you hungry for more!

Happy devouring!

Melissa Jeglinski

Melissa Jeglinski
Senior Editor
Silhouette Desire

Please address questions and book requests to:
Silhouette Reader Service
U.S.: 3010 Walden Ave., P.O. Box 1325, Buffalo, NY 14269
Canadian: P.O. Box 609, Fort Erie, Ont. L2A 5X3

THE LAWS
OF PASSION
LINDA CONRAD

Published by Silhouette Books
America's Publisher of Contemporary Romance

Special thanks and acknowledgment are given to Linda Conrad for her contribution to the DYNASTIES: THE DANFORTHS series.

This book is dedicated to romance lovers everywhere!
But especially to my supporters in the Rio Grande Valley of Texas:
Bill and Clare Braden along with so many others.
Thank you for everything!

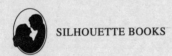 SILHOUETTE BOOKS

ISBN 0-373-76609-2

THE LAWS OF PASSION

Books by Linda Conrad

Silhouette Desire

The Cowboy's Baby Surprise #1446
Desperado Dad #1458
Secrets, Lies...and Passion #1470
*The Gentrys: Cinco #1508
*The Gentrys: Abby #1516
*The Gentrys: Cal #1524
Slow Dancing with a Texan #1577
The Laws of Passion #1609

**The Gentrys

LINDA CONRAD

was inspired by her mother, who first gave her a deep love of stories. "Mom told me I was the best liar she ever knew. And that's saying something for a woman with an Irish storyteller's background," she says. Linda was a stockbroker and certified financial planner but has been writing contemporary romances for six years now. Linda's passions are her husband, her cat, Sam, and finding time to read cozy mysteries and emotional love stories. Visit Linda's Web site at www.LindaConrad.com or write to her at P.O. Box 9269, Tavernier, FL 33070.

DYNASTIES: THE DANFORTHS

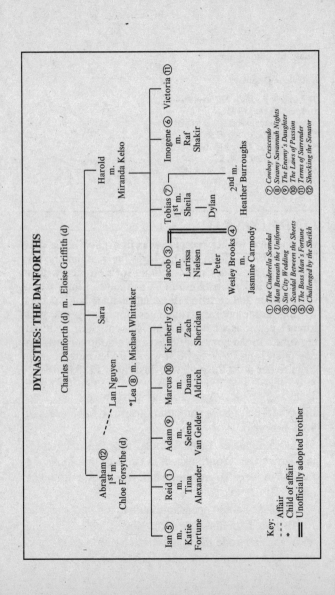

Charles Danforth (d) m. Eloise Griffith (d)

Sara

Harold
m.
Miranda Kelso

Abraham ⑫
1st m.
Chloe Forsythe (d)

Lan Nguyen
|
*Lea ⑧ m. Michael Whittaker

Reid ①
m.
Tina
Alexander

Adam ⑨
m.
Selene
Van Gelder

Marcus ⑩
m.
Dana
Aldrich

Kimberly ②
m.
Zach
Sheridan

Ian ⑤
m.
Katie
Fortune

Jacob ③
m.
Larissa
Nielsen
|
Peter

Wesley Brooks ④
m.
Jasmine Carmody

Tobias ⑦
1st m.
Sheila
|
Dylan

2nd m.
Heather Burroughs

Imogene ⑥
m.
Raf
Shakir

Victoria ⑪

① The Cinderella Scandal
② Man Beneath the Uniform
③ Sin City Wedding
④ Scandal Between the Sheets
⑤ The Boss Man's Fortune
⑥ Challenged by the Sheikh
⑦ Cowboy Crescendo
⑧ Steamy Savannah Nights
⑨ The Enemy's Daughter
⑩ The Laws of Passion
⑪ Terms of Surrender
⑫ Shocking the Senator

Key:
——— Affair
– – – Affair
* Child of affair
══ Unofficially adopted brother

Prologue

She'd be damned if some kid was going to tell her how to do her job.

No way was Dana Aldrich going to stand still for having this assistant's assistant insist she change into something more 'suitable'. As far as she was concerned, jeans were exactly right for this assignment. The newbie could just go do something useful…like… like… soak his head.

"Look, Special Agent Aldrich," the assistant continued unwarily. "Your suspect is accustomed to dating fashion models. To get him to talk you'd better look like one."

Before she could open her mouth to tell him what she really thought of his suggestions, the office door swung wide and in strode the man whose opinion she valued above all others. Special Agent-In-Charge, Steve

Simon, who was currently acting as the SAC for the Atlanta field office.

"SAC Simon, good to see you." She kept the excitement over seeing her old friend out of the tone in her voice.

"Are you having a problem, Special Agent Aldrich?"

"Not a bit, sir," she replied as she straightened up. "I'm just preparing for a new assignment and this yahoo wants to tell me how…"

"Excuse us a minute, Mr. Renuart." Steve shot Dana a quick look meant to keep her quiet while the administrative assistant took his leave.

"It's not like you to balk at instructions, Dana," Steve said, once the door was closed. "This new assignment you've drawn is politically sensitive. Marcus Danforth's father is an important businessman in this state. And he's also the front-running candidate for the U.S. Senate seat."

"I understand that," she told him. "But daddy Abraham Danforth's youngest son is not above the law. And Marcus Danforth should be the first to know it, too—considering that he's the corporate attorney for his family's company."

"Being accused of racketeering and being guilty are two different things, Dana. You know that."

She did know that very well. But she was also well aware that children of the extremely rich very often grew up spoiled. Maybe this one wanted to compete with his older brothers in the moneymaking department. And maybe he wanted it badly enough not to care how he went about it.

"What I know is that we've been trying to make a case

against this cartel. We've had informants tell us that they're using the coffee suppliers as a front for money laundering…and are probably using their shipping company to bring drugs into the country. But we can't prove it."

Steve nodded. "Every time we get close, an informant dies. That doesn't exactly make it easy to get others to tell us what they know."

"Well, if Marcus Danforth knows anything, I'll get to the truth." It was her job to find informants and offer them deals. "Is my cover all set?"

"Your credentials and backstory are on Renuart's desk. I've obtained the intro you'll need to stay close to Marcus." Steve stopped and put a hand on her shoulder. "Be vigilant, Dana. I'm not concerned about Marcus Danforth being violent. If anything, I truly believe his life might be in danger. But politics and drugs can be a deadly mixture."

He smiled at her. "And I don't want to lose my best undercover special agent."

"Don't worry," she said as she picked up her denim jacket. "As long as I don't have to wear spike heels, nothing is going to keep me from getting Danforth to roll over. That's my job and I'm the best at it."

Yep. Rich kid and Harvard grad, Marcus Danforth, had just better watch out. She was ready to go to work.

<u>One</u>

"**G**od, Adam, do I ever need a shower," Marc Danforth said, as he and his brother stepped out of the Chatham County Jail and strode toward the parking lot.

"We'll have you home in a jiffy." Adam handed him his coat jacket. "There seems to be a nip in the air all of a sudden. Sorry I had to park so far away."

Marc thought the early October air felt wonderful. Better than any air he'd ever breathed. He reveled in the ability to fill his lungs with the free oxygen.

"No sweat. I needed the walk anyway." Marc shrugged into his jacket. "I never figured a few hours in a jail cell could be so bad. I appreciate you coming to get me."

Marc felt a slight chill and stuffed both hands into his pockets. In one, he found the silk tie he'd been wearing yesterday—just where he'd left it. Well, at least the cops had an honest property system.

"No problem," Adam said. "Dad was here, too, most of the time. But when the reporters started showing up, I convinced him to slide out the backdoor. He said he'd talk to you later."

"I'll bet he's not real thrilled with me." Marc figured his father would probably be incensed that this arrest would cast his Senate campaign in a bad light.

"Ian is with him right now." Adam pulled his keys from his pocket and showed Marcus which way to walk toward the car. "It's clear to all of the family that this is a frame-up by the drug cartel. Ian's been fighting them off for nearly a year. First the threats, then that explosion and now this. Dad knows our battles have nothing to do with his campaign."

Marc nodded and breathed a sigh. Nothing much had mattered in his life for a long time. But family still mattered.

Family. He thought of the beautiful woman he'd met in his brother's office just a day earlier. He'd never seen Adam serious about a woman before, but he was willing to bet this relationship was going to last a while. "Does Selene know about my arrest?"

Adam smiled wryly. "I was with her when Dad called."

"Oh, hell." Marc blew out a weary breath, realizing what that meant. "A thousand apologies aren't going to be enough, are they?"

"Not nearly."

The tone almost made Marc laugh. Almost. A new thought struck, sobering him instantly. "It's…it's not possible that Selene's father is involved in this, is it?"

Adam shook his head. "Van Gelder certainly has his sleazy moments and dirty politics seems to be his way of life. But even *he* wouldn't stoop this low to win a Senate seat."

After a little thought, Marc was sure Adam was right. But his brain wasn't thinking too clearly right now. He was trying to stay confident that he would be found innocent of these made-up charges. But his career… hell…his whole life was on the line.

"Have you thought about hiring a high-profile lawyer?" Adam asked. "I mean, having your friend from the state Bar Association at your bond hearing was fine, but you're going to need a powerful criminal attorney to win this case."

Marc drove his hand through his greasy hair and winced. "The only thing I know for sure is that I won't be my own lawyer. I'm a damned good corporate counsel. But that doesn't mean I know anything about criminal law. Even if I did, the old saying that 'a man who hires himself as an advocate gets a fool for an attorney' is true."

"Well, Dad can suggest some good firms. And you have a few days to get yourself together before you worry about getting a lawyer."

"Like hell." Marc stopped in the middle of the parking lot and turned to his brother. "I intend to find the evidence that proves me innocent. I have to clear my name. And I have to do it before the drug cartel buries the information so deep I can never dig it out."

Suddenly he felt a determination that startled him. He'd been sleepwalking through his life for the last year, dedicating himself to his work and nothing else. But he didn't have that luxury anymore. No more feeling sorry for himself. His freedom depended on it.

Both brothers looked up as a car squealed around the

corner and headed down the parking lot lane toward where they were standing. Each of them absently backed up a step to let it pass.

The car slowed and stopped right in front of them. It was a late model four-door sedan. In Marc's opinion, the nondescript white, American-made vehicle looked just like an unmarked cop car should look. He groaned quietly and prepared himself for another hassle with the police.

The driver's door was on the far side away from them, so they couldn't see who was driving. While the car continued to idle, the door opened and out stepped a long, lanky female. Dressed in jeans, boots and a denim jacket, she looked serious and tough—except for the riot of curly black hair that hung halfway down her back.

If this was a cop, she might as well take him in right now. His thoughts could get him arrested—again.

All he could think of was being able to touch those soft, wild curls. Running his hands through that silk and burying his face in it as if it were an ebony pillow. He didn't suppose that was exactly what had brought her here, though.

"Marcus Danforth?" she asked in a whiskey-soft voice.

He closed his mouth and nodded. "That's me. And this is my brother, Adam. He doesn't have anything to do with these racketeering charges, however."

The woman walked around the front of the car and held out her hand. "Glad to meet you. The name's Dana Aldrich."

She shook his hand and then turned to Adam. While

she was shaking his brother's hand, Marc's fingers could still feel the strong, cool grasp of hers. And he wondered why anything so firm and businesslike should seem so erotic.

"Are you with the police?" Adam asked.

"No." She smiled at Adam but the cheer didn't reach her eyes. "I'm a private investigator. I work with your father's bodyguard, Michael Whittaker, on special cases. He's hired me to watch over your brother until the trial."

"What did you say?" Marc choked. This woman was definitely not what he thought of when someone said the word *bodyguard.* "I don't need a bodyguard. And no offense, Miss, but you don't look like the bodyguard type."

Adam ignored his remarks and asked a question of his own. "Can we see your ID, please?"

"Sure thing." She dug into her back pocket and came up with a leather case. "And I'm a damn good bodyguard, if I do say so myself."

Marc watched over his brother's shoulder while he studied the photos on both her state private investigator's license and driver's license. Adam handed them back.

"Give us a second, will you, Ms. Aldrich?" Adam took his elbow and escorted him down past three or four parked cars. "You buying this story of hers?" he inquired of Marc once they were out of earshot.

"Yeah, I guess so. Why would she lie?"

"Any number of reasons. In fact, she could be a tabloid reporter just looking for a good story."

Marc considered that possibility. "That's not what

my gut tells me. But if you're concerned, call Michael and ask him if he sent her. I'd be interested to know why he thinks I need a bodyguard. And why he would send me one that was such a knockout."

Adam grinned. "I'll do just that." He took his cell phone from its place on his belt clip. "You go back and keep her talking."

"No problem there. Take your time." As Marc walked toward her, he thought about what exactly having a female bodyguard might entail. And he wondered just how much of his body she might want to guard.

Dana glanced over her shoulder through the rear window and cut the wheel to the left. It was late for rush-hour traffic, but some of the roads were still clogged with cars.

"Are you hungry?" she asked Marcus, who sat quietly in the passenger seat beside her. "I thought we could stop somewhere and maybe miss some of this traffic."

As she drove onto the interstate, Dana relaxed her shoulders. It had been ridiculously easy to talk Marcus into letting her be his bodyguard. His brother, Adam, had been a little more leery, but he'd given in after he called Michael Whittaker and verified her story.

Adam wasn't the brother that interested her, however. She'd done a lot of research on Marcus Danforth for this assignment. But nowhere in the reams of paperwork about him did it say that he had fascinating chestnut eyes.

Or that his voice would be a dreamy baritone that brought out captivatingly sensual sensations in her. She shook her head a couple of times, trying to dislodge the strange impressions.

Her thoughts simply never turned to lustful cravings—never. She was too tough to allow such things. Clearly, she shouldn't think about that stuff when it came to a suspect. Marcus was a job, and she was a professional.

"I'm starved," he replied with a smile. "Fortunately, I didn't get a chance to eat jailhouse food. But, right now, all I want to do is go home. I think there might be some things in the refrigerator that'll be fresh enough to eat. I could fix us some eggs…after I take a shower, of course."

"Okay. That'll be fine. But you'll have to give me directions to your place."

"Just keep heading south for about twenty miles. I'll tell you when to get off the interstate."

Despite her momentary lapse into a ridiculously lust-filled haze over the man, her cover had held. Apparently, Steve had convinced his old army buddy, Michael, that the FBI wasn't simply out to prove Marcus guilty. An investigation might prove him innocent, as well.

And, moreover, it might be prudent to have a bodyguard around to help keep Marcus alive while he awaited his trial.

So she was in. But she intended to do everything in her power to find the evidence that would make the case hold. She felt sure this rich playboy lawyer was somehow involved in money laundering for the drug cartel.

She knew Marcus came from a very wealthy family with all the money in the world to hire legions of lawyers and private investigators. And Dana was determined to get to the evidence first so she would have a bargaining chip to help convince him to turn on his racketeering buddies and become an informer.

That is…if she could keep herself focused on the assignment and off Marcus's intense brown eyes.

Glancing into the rearview mirror, Dana caught sight of the same black SUV that she'd noticed earlier. "Hope you don't mind if we take a detour. Hang on." She whipped the wheel hard to the left and stepped down on the gas.

"What the hell?" Marcus jerked his head around to stare at her as she ripped in and out of traffic.

He cursed under his breath when she two-wheeled it past a car going seventy, hit the next exit ramp and locked the brakes. He struggled to balance himself on the seat while Dana maneuvered the boxy sedan down the ramp and blasted past the stop sign at the bottom.

She finally slowed down to the speed limit and looked around. "You have any idea of where we are?" she asked.

"That was some driving exhibition," he muttered. "What do you think you were doing?"

"Saving your butt. The driver of the car that was following us didn't look like any Sunday driver."

"A car was following us?"

Dana nodded, pulled into a convenience store's lot out by the air pumps and shut off the engine. "I understand you have some involvement with a drug cartel. I'm no expert, but I've seen the kind of cars those guys drive around town. A car like that had been following us since we pulled away from the jail. I figured it was time to shake them loose."

Was she kidding? "The drug cartel…why on earth would they be following me?"

"Maybe they're afraid you'll turn state's evidence

against your friends. Have the feds offered you a deal for information yet?"

He wiped the back of his hand across his mouth and tried to think. "I spent all morning in interrogation. But no one mentioned any deals. I got the distinct impression they already had plenty of evidence against me. At my arraignment, it sounded like the federal prosecutor's office wasn't interested in any more information…or any deals."

She'd turned in her seat to face him, and he noticed that her body seemed poised for action. Ready to fight or flee at any wrong move. Tense and in perfect control of herself and the situation. This was some bodyguard that Michael had hired.

Now that Marc's breathing was steadier, he decided to covertly study her, trying to remember everything she'd said. "Did you just say something about the cartel thinking I would turn on my *friends?* I don't have any connection to the cartel. I don't even *know* anyone that's in a cartel. Why would you think I did?"

"You were arrested for racketeering, weren't you?"

"Yes, but I'm *innocent.* I've been framed." Damn. The woman had the most gorgeous dark brown eyes he'd ever seen, but if she didn't believe in him… "Look, Dana. If you believe I'm guilty of what they say, maybe we'd better rethink this bodyguard deal."

She twisted in her seat and checked out the back window then turned the key in the ignition before she answered him. "I'm not paid to believe anything, pal. I'm a professional. It's my job to keep you alive."

Backing out of the space, she never looked at him, but her voice was strong. "You need a bodyguard and I'm the best. It doesn't matter what I think."

He laid a hand on her forearm. "It matters to me. Will you at least give me a chance to prove it to you?"

She stopped the car and stared down to where his hand touched her arm. "I'm just your bodyguard. I'll be right beside you until the trial. If you find any new information, I'll be there to see it." She glanced up and for a split second there was an odd expression on her face, then she tugged her arm out from under his hand.

In that instant he'd seen a different kind of emotion in her eyes. He'd begun to think of her as simply tough and beautiful. But buried deep in that gaze was something more.

Her expression reminded him of buried yearnings and crazy childish desires. It was totally out of context with the controlled and strong person he was beginning to know.

He'd seen a scared little girl buried deep in those eyes. A girl looking for someone who would love and care about her. It made him want to protect her. Made him want to insist she stop the car so he could change places and drive her around. Made him have a crazy vision of moving in front of her while bad guys pointed guns in her direction.

"So…" she began. "Let's get on with it."

The sexy, "tough guy" was back. And just that fast, Marc's protective impulses turned to something more primitive. Visions of her in bed, tangled up in his arms, appeared in his head.

"Yeah, okay. We'll talk about it." If he could manage to get past the pictures in his head—and also past some strong impulses a lot lower on his body, too.

"If I head south on this surface street, can we get to your place by the back roads?" she asked.

He nodded, but couldn't find his voice. Whoo boy. It had been a long time since he'd felt anything at all. Now suddenly he had tender images and sexual fantasies about a woman he'd just met?

These emotions must be originating from the events surrounding his arrest. Adrenaline, from fighting for his freedom, must be their root cause. He was just over stimulated, that's all.

Well, he had to put a lid on all of these powerful sensations. His life depended on being clear and focused.

And now that he thought about it a little more, Dana might be erotic as hell and have a body built for making love, but what did he really know about her? Something just didn't sit right. And he decided to find out what it was.

"This is your place?" Dana was thoroughly amazed.

She couldn't remember the last time anything had been a real surprise—well, if she didn't count her strange thoughts about kissing Marcus earlier.

Kissing? Was that what she'd wanted to do with him? In reality, she'd had no idea of where her lusting might lead. Having only just read and heard about most of that sexual stuff, she'd never experienced very much of it first hand. So the image of kissing a man she'd just met was odd.

"Yes. This is home. I can't tell you how grateful I am to see it again," he told her, while trying to conceal a sigh.

She shook off the images of putting her lips to his and looked through the windshield at the one-story ranch house, surrounded by grass and sitting in the middle of several acres of fenced land. It was much smaller than the house she'd imagined he would live in. And it was certainly smaller than the Danforth family's mansion, Crofthaven.

As she drove down the paved driveway, past fences and a few grazing animals, she tried to judge the house's size. With clean lines and stucco exterior, it seemed very suburban for a rich-man's son. It was probably a three or four bedroom home and it looked fairly new.

Really, she had no business thinking of a three-bedroom house as small. Although not a mansion; compared to the rat-infested twelve-by-twelve room in Atlanta where she'd grown up, this place would qualify as a castle.

"What do you do with all this space?" She'd checked out the sea of grass that was the front yard, enclosed by both chain-link fence and pretty white-wood fence posts, and now saw a building in the distance that might be a garage or a barn in back of the main house.

He chuckled at her question. "It's not much, I know. But it's a farm. My farm."

"You mean you grow stuff here? Like fruit and vegetables that come out of the ground? Really?"

She pulled up in front of the house and stopped. Turning to see why he hadn't answered her yet, Dana was shocked by the wide grin on his face. It made him look so appealing that she nearly threw herself into his arms.

He chuckled, and she straightened her spine.

"I've got a couple of peach trees," he said cheerfully. "So I guess that qualifies as fruit. Last summer I grew tomatoes and zucchini and tried growing one stalk of corn. Maybe you could count those as vegetables."

Again he chuckled, but this time it seemed more like he was laughing at himself. "Mostly I raise a few sheep and some chickens. It's not a very big operation but I'm happy here." He opened his door and, unfolding his tall frame from the front seat, he stepped out and stretched.

"Oh. Farm animals," she said, with what she figured was a truly stupid look on her face.

Everything she knew about farming you could put in a teacup. A small one. She never figured that a rich guy like this would like living the country life. All of a sudden her investigator's instincts kicked in.

In the long haul, she never trusted what she saw at first glance. And over her lifetime, she'd come to realize that rich people couldn't be trusted if it was a question of making money. So this whole domestic scene made her wary and nervous. What was he really doing way out here in the boondocks?

Dana slipped the key from the ignition and carefully got out of the car. The sunset was casting shadows against the house and shrubbery. Nervous and wondering who else might be around, she turned to lock the car and immediately heard a crazy commotion behind her.

Before she could turn back to see what was going on, Marcus yelled, "Dana! Watch out!"

She swiveled, pulled her revolver out of its holster

and grasped it firmly in her hand before she made the full turn.

"No! For God's sake, Dana. Don't shoot him."

The next thing she knew, she was flat on the ground, staring up at a ferocious set of snarling teeth.

Two

"Laddie, heel!" Marcus shouted. "Get off of her, you big lummox."

Dana rolled out from under the collie and got to her feet. She checked her weapon and reholstered it while the oversize dog sat on his haunches, wagging his tail and breathing hard.

"I'm sorry about that," Marcus quickly told her. "Are you hurt?"

"I'm fine. What made him jump me that way? Is he a guard dog? I've never heard of anyone using a collie for that kind of thing."

"Laddie? No. He's a big wimp. But he's good with the sheep." Marcus bent low to rub the dog's head and gave him a quick hug. "Did you miss me, boy?"

Marcus stood and turned back to Dana. "He's really just a big puppy. I've tried to train him not to jump up on visitors, but obviously we have some more work to do."

She lowered her chin and nodded once. "Right. Well, no harm done."

He took a second to study her again. Dana was much more than just a bodyguard. Marc was sure of it.

"That was some quick action with the gun, slick," he chided her. "Where'd you learn to draw like that?"

Dana adjusted her jacket down over the holster again before she answered. "Would you believe anyone can do that with a lot of practice?"

He narrowed his eyes at her.

"No? I guess you wouldn't," she sighed. "Let's just say that handling weapons is one of my many talents."

"Uh-huh. And driving is another one of your many talents?" The minute he said it, his mind wandered off to what other kind of talents she might possess. Or which ones he could bring out in her...if he had a chance to do all the things with her that he'd been imagining.

"I learned to drive that way in bodyguard training. It's a good thing to know if you anticipate a potential kidnapping."

That stopped the images. "Do you anticipate a kidnapping?"

She shook her head. "It's not something a bodyguard can ever ignore. But in this case, I think that an execution-style killing might be more likely. Either way, we'll be prepared." She headed toward the front door.

Man. Talk about throwing a wet blanket on his ardor. "I'll open up the house for you and give you a quick tour, but then I have to see to the animals," he finally managed after swallowing hard a couple of times.

Her eyes widened and her brows shot up. "You take care of them yourself?"

"Sure I do. Who else?" He suddenly thought back on the last couple of days. "Well, there is my neighbor who looks after them if I'm gone. He's a full-time farmer, not a hobby farmer like most of the rest of us around here."

"I need to stay with you while you tend your animals," she told him. "If you want to do that before you clean up, then I'll go with you. What exactly do you have to do?"

She was too much, this tough cookie with curly soft hair and a spine made of steel. Intelligent and athletic to be sure. But she also had a tiny hint of softness behind those big brown eyes.

"You'll see." Marc unbuttoned the top button on his shirt and threw his jacket over the little bench beside the front door.

Then he turned to Laddie. "Come on boy. Time to work for your supper."

As they walked toward the sheep pasture, he began to wonder about Dana and her background. "Have you ever had a pet to take care of?"

"Never. I don't have time for such things."

"Not even when you were a kid?"

She looked away and hesitated, apparently trying to decide how much of herself she was willing to reveal.

At last she gave in and shrugged her shoulders. "Where I was raised, animals were too much of a luxury. I knew a couple of kids from the block who had dogs." Her eyes were dark and stormy. "But my father always used to say pets were a waste of money and that their families would be better off eating them rather than feeding them."

Marc winced at the thought. "Where were you raised?"

"Somewhere far removed from where *you* were brought up," she replied with sarcastic fervor. "Not all of us are lucky enough to have mansions and luxuries while we're growing up. The place where we lived was smaller than one of your guest bathrooms, I'm sure."

"Hey. Take it easy. I didn't mean to insult you. It's just that the thought of eating a pet is a little hard for me. I have enough trouble thinking that someday I'll have to sell off some of my sheep. So far, all I've managed to do is have a man come in to shear them in the spring."

"My father…thought about things a lot differently than your average man." A couple of beats went by in silence. "So, you think of your sheep as pets?" she asked with an abrupt change of topic.

"I try not to, but sometimes it isn't easy to treat them like a business proposition, either."

They'd arrived at the gate between pasture and pen. Marc swung open the gate and whistled for Laddie to get around behind the small herd and begin moving them toward the pen.

"Come on," he urged her. "I'll show you how to set out their feed. And then you can learn how to clean out a chicken coop. Won't that be fun?"

She threw him such an incredulous look that he had to laugh. Wherever she'd grown up, she certainly hadn't been raised on a farm.

But the surprise was that she was willing to get her

hands dirty. She dug right into the chores. He'd never met a woman quite like her.

Dana was so far removed from the last woman in his life that it was almost a joke. Nothing, however, about that miserable affair had been a bit funny.

Dana took the last dish from Marcus, dried it and put it in the cabinet. She turned and watched him clean the counters. He was such an intense kind of guy that this domestic scene seemed slightly off.

While he'd been in the shower, she'd done a cursory search of the house. No one else was here at the moment and, judging by the absence of anyone else's personal effects, he lived alone. She hadn't had the time to go through his papers or files, but she'd noted that his answering machine had an even dozen messages blinking.

She wanted to find out more about him, before she did anymore digging. "Whatever made you decide to live on a hobby farm?"

When he turned to her with a slightly embarrassed smile, she felt a lump forming in her throat. She couldn't figure out why the handsome and outgoing man's sudden red flush should bother her so much. But she felt her own pink-tinged blush rushing up from her chest and spreading over her neck and face.

He looked good enough to eat for dessert. His hair was still wet from the shower and had darkened to a deep coffee color. He'd changed into a pair of jeans. No shirt. No shoes. Just a worn pair of work jeans.

His well-earned muscles rippled with the slight sheen of sweat, making her want to touch him—to learn the ins and outs of every crevice on his body. He was the first man that had ever made her tremble at the sight of a bare chest.

But she couldn't allow herself to dwell on his formidable body, she chided herself. He was her suspect and a potential informer. She had to play this smart.

"I don't quite know how to answer you," he replied. "I work hard at my job and don't have many hobbies…anymore. I bought this place a couple of years ago because I thought it would make a good place to raise a family."

He hung up his dish towel and sat on a stool at the kitchen counter. "About a year ago I…uh…changed my mind about the family. But then I thought the place seemed lonely without youngsters around, so I bought a few lambs. And here we are—a real working farm."

"You don't mind the work?"

"Not at all. It relaxes me. I've found I love to work the ground and care for the animals. It's so basic. So elemental and idyllic. And a small place like this doesn't take much time."

She hung up her own towel. "I like working my body hard too. When I'm concentrating on the work, the rest of the world disappears. It's quite powerful."

"Exactly." Marc tried not to react to her words, but the image of her working her powerful body while on top of his body just wouldn't go away.

The silence between them was tense for a minute.

Finally, Dana broke the ice. "I checked your security system while you were in the shower. It's a fairly good system. It should keep you safe."

He couldn't help but chuckle. "I had it installed when I moved in, but I keep forgetting to set the darn thing."

"Not while I'm on the case, you won't."

"Will you be staying here with me?" It hadn't occurred to him that this was a twenty-four hour a day job.

"Of course. Kidnappers and assassins don't exactly operate in broad daylight or when it's convenient for you."

"But I'm going to be…uh…searching for evidence to prove my innocence." He didn't want anyone around if he had to break into someone's office looking for evidence.

"Not a problem. I'll be right there with you."

"But…"

She didn't let him finish his sentence, but waved him off instead. "That's my job. I intend to keep you alive until the trial. And I don't care what it takes."

He thought she was the most adorable "tough guy" he'd ever laid eyes on. If he was really in more danger than merely being framed, he couldn't have picked a better person to watch over him.

"Do you receive mail out here?" she asked.

"No. I have everything sent to my office."

"That's good. It might take them a little while to figure out where you live. We have some time."

"Time? Time for what?" Now if that wasn't a leading question, he didn't know what was. But he knew exactly where he *wanted* it to lead.

"To prepare ourselves for an attack…more than just the alarm system. Do you own any weapons?"

"Guns? No way. I've always figured that in case of a break in, I'd probably get shot with my own gun."

"How about Laddie? Will he bark if someone comes around to let us know there's danger?"

"Hmm." He thought of the overgrown, fluffy puppy and grinned. "Maybe. If we can keep him out of the house. He likes to sleep on the suede sofa. And he's a pretty heavy sleeper, too."

Dana threw her hands on her hips and grimaced. "For crying out loud. Haven't you ever considered the possibility of a kidnapping before? You're a wealthy and intelligent man, Marcus. That sort of thing can easily happen if you don't pay attention."

An unwelcome memory snuck up and jabbed him. "Yeah, I know that. One of my cousins disappeared a few years back. Victoria was a pain in the neck when we were kids, but she had turned into quite a beautiful teenager. The family figured when she was missing for a while that it was a kidnapping, but no ransom demand was ever made."

"Disappeared? Was she ever found?"

He slowly shook his head. "Maybe she just ran away from home. But I doubt it. She didn't seem unhappy." Marc stood and stretched. "I guess I have been a little careless. But somehow you just don't think things like that can ever happen to you."

"Well then, I'd like to suggest that we spend no more time here at your farm than we have to. I'll go out in a while and move my car out of sight. I'll put it into the barn next to your SUV for the night. And we'll keep the drapes drawn and lights dim. Tomorrow we can make other arrangements. All right?"

"Yes, I guess so. I do have the animals to worry about, however. But maybe I can ask my neighbor to keep an eye on them again."

"Good idea. And I think you should let your answering machine pick up all your calls from now on." Dana stood and shook the kinks out of her arms and legs.

She looked like a raw bundle of energy packaged into a long and beautiful body. The very air around her shivered with the powerful and electric vibes she threw off. Man, would he like to capture a little of that energy. She seemed so vital and sensual.

Marc couldn't remember lusting after a woman the way he'd been lusting after Dana...not since...way back as a horny teenager. He'd been aroused since the first moment he'd seen her standing in the parking lot.

"By the way," she interrupted his thoughts. "When I was checking your security, I noticed that you had a few phone messages on your answering machine. Maybe you should listen to them so you can clear the machine for more."

"I imagine that's my family wondering how I'm holding up after my *unfortunate incarceration.*"

"You have a big family, don't you?"

"Enormous. There were five kids in my immediate family. And my aunt and uncle have four kids...plus a great guy they took in, who seems like just another brother now."

He headed toward the den, but kept talking over his shoulder. "A couple of months ago we found out about an adult sister that none of us had known anything about. And just lately we've had a rash of weddings and engagements, adding spouses and potential spouses, with kids and babies coming along faster than you can think."

"Whew! How do keep them all straight?" She tagged behind him down the hall.

"It's easy when you're born into it. I'm not sure how all the newcomers are going to get along with everyone else, though." Marc flipped on the light in the den and went to his desk. "Do you have any siblings? Or were you lucky enough to be an only child?"

Dana wasn't sure how to answer that. Just how much of herself did she dare lay open to him? Strangely enough, she really wanted to tell him the truth about herself.

This wasn't a deep undercover operation. She'd been on several of those in the past. But her boss was convinced that Marcus was truly just a pawn of the drug cartel's and not a major player in their operation.

Her job here was to find a way into Marcus's confidence so that he would turn over any evidence he might have and then testify against the cartel in court. The more she was around him and the better she began to know him, though, the less she wanted to be undercover at all.

There were some things about the man that intrigued her. Things like a deeply injured look in his eyes that appeared whenever he thought no one was watching.

So…was he on the take from the mob? After all, the state's attorney thought there was enough evidence against him to charge him with racketeering. But something about him—maybe it was the gentle way he had with his animals, or the rough and hungry looks he'd been throwing in her direction—just didn't seem like most of the criminals she'd known in the past.

She'd been so sure at first that he was a spoiled rich man's son who'd signed on with the bad guys to get what he wanted. Her training led her to make quick judgments about people and get to their real motives later.

Sometimes a special agent had to make life and death decisions based only on a cursory observation. And she had been observing Marcus—a lot. Now she just didn't know what to think.

As the silence began to grow awkward, she opted to tell him the truth. "I was an only child. My parents are both dead now. I'm all the family I've got." She took a moment and made a snap decision to trust him with another small piece of herself. "I like the solitary life. I've never been impressed with the way most families interact."

Marcus scowled at her. "Not even your own?"

"Especially my own."

He stepped closer, lifted a hand and grazed the line of her jaw with a knuckle. "That's a sad commentary, Dana. It can be a wonderful thing to know there are people who care about you no matter what."

A soft and concerned look moved into his eyes. Up this close, she could smell his tangy, fresh-sage scent and feel the heat emanating from his bare chest.

He kept on gently stroking her face and gazing into her eyes. Soothing and stirring. She felt her pulse begin to jackhammer and her senses went on hyperalert.

When he leaned closer and his eyes zeroed in on her mouth, the heat between them exploded. With a shake of her head, she caught herself before she fell into his arms. She had to remember that he was just part of the job.

Dana took a step back and averted her eyes toward

his desk. She'd never before given herself over to a man. And she would definitely not be starting with someone who was a suspect in a case she was working.

"You'd better check your messages," she said in a raspy voice. "Is it too warm in here for you?"

The dreamy look disappeared from his eyes, but he smiled and cocked his head toward her. "You're hot? Why don't you take off some of those clothes."

Okay. She might be a virgin, but she wasn't totally naive. That was a come-on she'd heard often enough before.

She rolled her shoulders and narrowed her eyes at him. "Just check your messages. I'll be fine."

He shrugged a shoulder, but the smile stayed put as he turned to punch the Play button on the machine.

The first couple of messages were from various family members asking him if he needed anything and to please call if he wanted company or a place to stay. The distress and genuine concern in their voices was quite evident.

Dana wasn't sure how such obvious love amongst family members made her feel. It was an interesting side note to Marcus's character profile. But deeper than that, and on a personal level, it almost made her feel…lonely.

"Marc? We need to talk." A deep voice boomed out of the machine. "I just got a call from…well, it was about you. And it's important that we discuss this as soon as possible. I'll be at the office until ten or eleven o'clock tonight. I'd rather not talk about it over the phone, so why don't you come over? Give me a call."

The message clicked off and Marcus touched the button on his machine that erased the previous messages.

"Who was that?" she asked. If it was one of the cartel members, this might be the break she'd been waiting for.

"That was my brother, Ian."

"It was? He sounded worried."

"Yeah, he did, didn't he?"

"Is he the one that heads up the family company?"

Marcus nodded. "I think I'd better go to the office and talk to him. Do you mind?"

Suddenly, it struck Dana that maybe their entire company was a front for the cartel. Were they all involved in money laundering? Perhaps the family was using Marcus as a scapegoat.

"I don't mind at all," she said. "In fact, I insist."

"Great. I'll go throw on a shirt and see you later." He picked up his keys off the desk and started for the door.

"Hold on." She grabbed his arm and swung him around. "You don't go anywhere without me, remember? Like it or not, from now until your trial we're stuck with each other as if we'd been put together with Crazy Glue. Get used to it."

Three

Was he glad that Dana had insisted on coming along to the office? He couldn't quite settle his thoughts when it came to her. But they were both about to leave for his meeting with Ian, just the same.

He wanted her to trust him and believe in him, though he had no idea why. But would she inhibit his efforts to prove himself innocent? He sighed, resigned to having her company whether he wanted it or not.

"How about if we take my SUV and I'll drive?" he asked, as they locked the front door and set the alarm system.

She shook her head and headed for the driver's side of her small, bland sedan. "No thanks. You don't have the training, and the whole world already knows what kind of car you normally drive. In the protection business, the idea is to vary your routine…change cars, times and the routes to your regular haunts."

Well, Marc had certainly found one thing he was not happy about. He didn't like riding in her car. He wanted to drive himself around like usual, and he liked his normal routine. This whole business was really starting to suck.

He directed her to the Danforth corporate office building via the back roads and downtown side streets. The parking lot was all but empty at this time of night. A security van patrolled the exterior grounds and Ian's car was parked in his normal spot.

"Nice office," Dana said as she parked the car where he'd directed. "These brick buildings that are so common in old Savannah are very efficient. And I imagine all the trees and flowers make a nice impression on clients. Do you have many muggings or break ins in this part of town?"

He opened his car door and "tsked" at her. "You look at a beautiful historic building and fantastically lush landscaping and think of muggings? You've been in the bodyguard business too long, Ms. Aldrich." He breathed deep and took in the sweet smell of honeysuckle that he'd loved since he was a kid.

She shrugged her shoulders, climbed out and locked her car. "To be the best at my job, you have to work at it twenty-four hours a day. Everything I see has some significance to the…uh…protection business. I don't pay attention to the superficial things in this world."

"You never take any time off to just enjoy yourself— to smell the flowers?" He slid his key into the door lock at the employee entrance and opened it. "What's that old saying about all work and no play…?"

She grimaced and stepped ahead of him into the darkened downstairs hallway. "I don't mind being dull. The job has all the excitement I need."

While he led her down the hall toward the elevator behind reception, his heels clicked loudly against the polished-pecan floors. Again, Marc began to wonder about the intelligent and strong woman who'd become his bodyguard. Just what kind of person was she?

There seemed to be so much hidden about her. Did she have any kind social of life? Like, for instance, a husband or a boyfriend somewhere? When she'd talked about not caring much for family, he'd thought she had only meant her parents. Now he was becoming convinced that she was a real loner. With no one in her life who mattered.

And it was becoming very important to him to figure her out. If she'd let him, he wanted to be the one to show her how to relax and enjoy herself. To appreciate history and learn to see the beauty of the world around her. She was beginning to matter. But for the life of him, he couldn't pin down the reason he cared so much.

That kind of reflection would have to come after he'd cleared his name. And kept himself out of jail. First things first.

The elevator reached the fifth floor and they stepped out onto the Persian carpet runner and headed in the direction of the CEO's office. Marcus pointed out his own office down the hall the other way.

Ian was waiting for them at his desk. He stood when they came in and shot Marcus a wary glance.

"Ian, this is my new bodyguard, Dana Aldrich."

"Yes, I heard all about her from Adam." Ian turned to her. "How do you do, Ms. Aldrich. Michael Whittaker tells me he doesn't know you personally, but he speaks quite highly of your reputation. Thank you for taking this job on such short notice."

She shook his hand. "I'm glad to help."

"Good." Ian turned back to his desk. "Now, if you don't mind, I have a few things to say to my brother in private. You may wait in my reception area. I don't think there'll be any attempts on Marc's life while he's in my office."

Dana straightened her spine and stood her ground. She turned to Marcus for his word on the matter. Marcus looked hesitant but didn't jump in to ask her to stay.

"I won't be in your way, Mr. Danforth," she insisted to Ian. "But I believe a good bodyguard should know where all the threats are coming from. If what you have to say to Marcus pertains to his arrest or the charges against him, I'd like to be made aware of it at the same time."

"Yes, Ian. I want her to stay," Marcus finally urged. "She's going to be with me as I find the evidence to prove my innocence. She might as well know what we're up against."

Ian laid a hand on his arm. "All right, baby brother. I guess you need as many people on your side as you can get right now. If that's what you want, she can stay. Both of you have a seat."

Ian eased into his huge leather chair and drove his fingers through his hair. "You're not going to like what I have to say."

Marcus leaned his big six-two frame toward the front

of the high-backed visitor's chair. "What's wrong? Is it the family? Are they all okay?"

"Yes," Ian told him. "Everyone is fine at the moment. Everyone but you."

"It's not Dad then? He can't be happy about my arrest when he's just about to swing this election. He's still running ahead, isn't he?"

"Dad's not concerned about how your arrest will or will not affect his election chances. He's concerned about you. We all are." Ian hesitated a moment, then bit his lip.

Dana was astounded. Everything she'd ever read or heard about Ian Danforth said he was the self-assured and competent president of a national firm. But at the moment, he looked stung and unsure of himself. She sat back and waited to hear his story.

"I had a phone call a little while ago, Marc. From…"

"Don't tell me. I'll bet it was from our nemesis, Sonny Hernandez. I don't have any doubts that he's in on this frame-up. What did he want?"

"Excuse me," Dana interrupted. "I know I said I'd just be quiet, but who's this Sonny Hernandez?"

Marcus turned to her. "He a scum gopher for a drug cartel and a local coffee bean importer. Nasty piece of work he is, too. He's been pressuring us to do business with the importer exclusively."

"What kind of business?"

"He doesn't just want to do business with our shipping company," Ian told her. "He wants our help with laundering their dirty drug money."

"Ah. Drug dealing is nasty stuff. What kind of pressure?" she asked, in as innocent tone of voice as she could manage.

"The threats started back in February," Marcus replied. "Then in April they got a lot more personal when they blew up one of our warehouse offices."

"Blew it up? An explosion? Was anyone hurt?" Dana had read about it in the files, but she wanted their take on who had done it.

Ian shook his head. "No. And so far the police haven't found any clues as to who set it off. But we know who's behind it."

"You mean you think the importers blew up your building to coerce you into doing what they want?"

Ian scowled. "Yes and no. Yes, the explosion was meant to scare me into doing what they want. But no, it's not coming from the local coffee bean people. Like Marc was saying, they're just a front for a Colombian drug cartel. The cartel has threatened my life several times, and went so far as kidnapping an innocent woman who they mistook for my mistress. And when those tactics didn't work, they framed my brother."

Marcus stirred in his chair then addressed Ian. "So what did good old charming Sonny have to say tonight?"

"It wasn't Sonny this time," Ian told him. "The call was from the kingpin himself. Ernesto Estoban Escalante."

Dana's jaw dropped opened, but she covertly closed it and swallowed hard. Escalante? The most notorious drug lord in the world? The FBI had been hunting the man for nearly a decade. Every time they thought they had him, he'd drop back into the oblivion of the Colombian rain forests where his cartel ruled supreme.

And he had personally called Ian Danforth tonight? Suddenly everything changed for Dana. If what Ian and Marcus had told her was true, the Danforths were in big trouble. And she had stepped into something much larger than Marcus and his racketeering charge.

But she still wasn't positive that the Danforths were innocents. What if Marcus had given in to the cartel to protect his brother? He could still make a good informant.

Dana kept her mouth shut and listened.

Ian was speaking to Marcus and shaking his head sadly. "I don't know how to fix this for you, Marc. Escalante plainly told me that if I would help them launder their money through the coffee supplies that he'd get you off the hook. But…"

"The bastard as much as admitted to you that he framed me?" Marcus snapped.

"Yeah. I thought I'd lived through the worst they could throw at me. But…I can't sit back and let you go to jail for something you didn't do." Ian grimaced and took a breath. "Besides, they won't stop at that. Next they'll probably start murdering all of us…one at a time."

"You can't be thinking of giving in to them now?" Marcus sounded stunned. "You can't do that. I'm not going to jail for something I didn't do. Don't worry. I'll find the evidence to prove my innocence. Just give me a little time."

Dana just had to interrupt again to make a comment. "By any chance did you happen to get tonight's phone call on tape?"

Ian narrowed his eyes at her. "I don't normally tape my phone conversations, no."

"Are you going to try getting the police involved

with this again?" Marcus asked his brother. "They have to believe you by now."

"They do believe us. But there's nothing they can do without proof. All the leads we've given them have turned cold. The cartel is too powerful." Ian took a deep breath and ran the back of his hand across his mouth. "And too dangerous. I'm not going to let any more of my family suffer out of some misguided sense of righteousness. I can't. It's not worth it."

"Ian, please," Marcus begged. "Give me at least a few days to find the proof. I promise you, I'm not going to jail…and we'll find the evidence to stop this once and for all."

Ian clenched his fists on his desk. Then he turned to Dana. "Can you guarantee me that you'll keep him alive while he investigates this damned murdering drug lord?"

Dana hesitated for one second then answered him sharply. "I can guarantee you that as long as I am alive, Marcus will be fine. Nothing will happen to him."

"Yeah? Well, I'd just as soon you didn't die over my stupid pride, either." Ian stood and started to pace. "All right, Marc," he finally agreed. "I can put them off for a couple more weeks. But after that I give up. You are not going to do time for a crime you didn't commit. Not as long as I can stop it."

Marcus stood and went to put a hand on his brother's shoulder. "Don't worry, Ian. We'll beat them." He turned and smiled at Dana. "And I'll be all right. I have a guardian angel at my side."

Dana stood, too. "I've never been called an angel before." She set her jaw and turned to Ian. "But don't worry, Mr. Danforth. I intend to see that all of you come out of this in one piece. You have my word."

As both men stood speechless after that strange remark, Dana's mind was already leaping into a plan. "Okay. Now. What can you tell me about your phone system? And after we check on that, I want you to tell me everything you remember about that phone call with Escalante."

Marc checked to see that the employee door was locked as they left the office building. Then he followed a very antsy Dana while she cautiously climbed into her car and pressed the door-lock button as soon as he'd closed the door behind him.

She put her key in the ignition, but didn't turn it. "There's something I have to tell you," she said softly.

"I had a feeling there might be."

She looked at him out of the corner of her eye and shifted slightly in her seat. "Yeah, you're too smart not to have been guessing about me. And I'd also be willing to bet that Ian is on the phone to Michael Whittaker right this minute, demanding some answers."

"You're not a bodyguard, are you?"

She shook her head.

"Then who…?"

"I'm an FBI special agent, Marcus. I've been assigned to offer you a deal to turn over any information that could help the federal attorney convict the cartel."

"FBI agent?" After his initial shock, he knew in his gut that what she'd said was true. "I suppose you can prove that?" he asked anyway.

"Not at the moment. I've been undercover…you understand. But I want to take you to someone who can prove it for me. He's someone I think you should talk to."

"Just a minute." Marc's mind was swimming with all the things she'd said. "Why are you telling me this now? What's changed?"

"I've changed. I don't think you're guilty of racketeering anymore."

"Gee, thanks." He reached over and took her chin in his hand, forcing her to look at him. "You mean when I first told you I wasn't guilty you thought I was lying?"

She pulled her chin from his grip, but turned in her seat to face him. "That's how I was trained. Suspect everyone and trust no one. It isn't personal. It's just my job."

Not personal? And here he'd been dreaming of making things between them as personal as you can get. He still wanted that. In fact, his fingers ached right now with wanting to touch her again.

"Okay, Dana. Let's go see the man who can prove who you are." This revelation of hers was going to take a bit of getting used to.

She bent to crank the ignition, but he suddenly thought of something and stopped her. "Hey. *Dana Aldrich* is your real name, isn't it?"

"It's the name I've always used," she told him flatly. "That's all I can tell you."

Marc sat in stony silence while Dana drove them all over town, ending up only a few blocks from where they'd started. She'd made two mobile-phone calls, but he didn't catch much from her side of the conversation.

A war was going on inside him. He was mad. Confused. Slightly frightened and…still desperate to find a way into Dana's bed. She was totally different than any woman he'd ever known. And he'd never figured that he would be so attracted to a tough, professional law-woman.

In fact, he never figured he would be attracted to any woman ever again after that monumentally embarrassing fiasco of last year. Yet, here he was, lusting after a woman with long, soft curls and the biggest brown eyes he'd ever seen.

They finally pulled into a darkened garage behind a nondescript building on East Bryan Street and parked the car. "Where are we?" he asked.

"The FBI Resident Agency office. Luckily, my boss is here in Savannah from the Atlanta field office. I want him to meet you."

They climbed the back stairs to the fourth floor. "The office is open at this hour?" he asked.

She shook her head and led him into a shadowed hallway. "The public reception area closes at five. We're headed to a small conference suite in back."

Dana opened a door for him to walk through. As he stepped inside, he saw a medium sized room, absolutely crammed with high-tech equipment. When his eyes adjusted to the dim light, he recognized state-of-the-art computers and a screen that seemed to be some kind of radar scanner. A young man was sitting in front of communications-style machines that blinked with lights and buzzed with noises.

But Dana didn't acknowledge the man who was operating the computers. She walked right past the guy.

"This way." Dana motioned Marc to follow her into

a side room. "Good evening, SAC Simon," she said as she closed the door.

"Dana." A middle-aged man with steel blue eyes and a little gray at his temples stood and walked toward them. "And this must be Marcus Danforth. I'm Special Agent-In-Charge Steve Simon. Please just call me Steve." He shook hands. "How're you doing?"

"I'm not so hot, at the moment," Marc grumbled. "This morning I was in jail, and tonight I seem to have been dropped into some kind of weird espionage movie. I'm not thrilled about either one."

"Have a seat, son. I think we'd better talk." Steve moved to the polished wood conference table and took a chair.

When the three of them were seated, Marc couldn't wait to start asking questions. "Why am I here? What do you want from me?"

"You're here in our covert operations office because Dana has disobeyed standard procedures and told you who she really is," Steve replied. "You are also here because you may be able to help both your family and your country. Are you willing to listen to and then consider a proposition to do both of those things?"

Marc nodded his head but kept his mouth shut. He wasn't sure how he'd gotten himself into this mess, but now he knew he needed advice on how to get out of it.

"Good. But first, I want to assure you that the woman you've known as your bodyguard is indeed Special Agent Dana Aldrich. I've already received a call from my old friend, Michael Whittaker, saying your brother Ian is determined to find out the truth about her. I'll call Ian later and explain. We'll probably be needing his assistance on this investigation anyway."

Steve sat back in his chair and studied both Marc and Dana. "I understand your brother received a phone call tonight from Ernesto Escalante. If he is determined to get your family's assistance in his schemes, there is no way you can escape his wrath. He's one of the most dangerous men on earth. So far you have all been very lucky."

"Lucky? I wouldn't say that what we've been through qualifies as anything but bad luck." Marc gritted his teeth in frustration. "Don't tell me there's no hope of besting the cartel. I refuse to believe it. I intend to get the proof I need to beat my frame-up."

Steve smiled at him. "I believe you would try it. But you might die trying. And then what? Escalante would just keep the pressure on Ian to do what he wants. Killing off your family members one by one would be his next move."

"That's what Ian said." Marcus was annoyed as hell now. There had to be a way out of this.

"Your brother is a smart man who's been in a terrible bind. But I have an idea for something that might end your family's terror right here. Will you listen?"

Marc sat up in his chair and looked from Dana to Steve and back again. "I'll listen."

Steve spent the next hour outlining a plan for him and Dana to investigate the whereabouts of Escalante and then for them to participate in a sting designed to capture the man and put an end to the blackmail once and for all. Marc wasn't positive the plan would work. But he figured it was worth a shot. After all, he was the one family member that now had nothing to lose.

It was two a.m. when he and Dana left the FBI office and climbed back into her car. "Does this car really belong to you?" he inquired as he stifled a yawn.

"It's a Bureau vehicle," she told him. "It has a few modifications over the standard issue. It'll do sixty in eight seconds flat. There are airbags across the front and on all doors."

She smiled as they buckled up. "And it's also equipped with a transmitter and GPS positioner that will work in a radius of up to three hundred miles."

"Terrific." Marc was becoming more irritable by the second. Regardless of being warned by her boss to obey Dana's instructions at the risk of his life, he was tired and still furious that Dana had lied to him. Oh, he knew it was her job, but still…

"Where are we headed?" he scowled.

"To your farm. Now that I know for sure you're not involved with the cartel, I'm convinced they have no reason to take you out…yet. They need you alive, temporarily, to use as a hold over Ian. So we should be fairly safe at your home for a while."

Dana backed out of the garage and headed down the river road in the general direction of the farm. "Besides, you look like you're about to drop. We'll be able to form a clearer strategy after you get a good night's sleep."

Marc stewed in silence for the entire forty-five minutes it took them to travel what should've been a twenty-minute trip. Evidently, she was never going to drive in a straight line to any destination.

When they arrived, she pulled in behind the barn and they got out as she locked the doors. "I'll check your SUV for bugs and tracking devices in the morning. We may need to use it as part of the sting."

"Swell." He grabbed her arm and swung her around

to face him. "You owe me something. You've admitted you lied, and I want to know how many of the things you told me were true and what was just part of the game."

In the clear light of a full moon, he saw her face flush with anger and her hands ball into fists. "I told you…it was all part of the job."

She tried to jerk herself free from his grasp, but he tightened his grip. "No dice, sister. That's not going to cut it anymore. I want to know who you are—underneath the tough special agent."

"Don't make a huge mistake before we even get started, Danforth. You're asleep on you feet. It'll all look better in the morning."

"Maybe so, sugar. But I'm still going to want answers."

She was right. It was a mistake to take out all his frustrations on her. But what the hell? He'd been dying to get his hands on her since the first instant she'd spoken his name in that spun-sugar voice of hers. And now he could feel her muscled upper arm flexing under his hand.

He wanted to touch her skin without the clothes. He wanted to see what she looked like standing naked before him. He wanted…

"Take your hand off me." She slipped her keys into her pocket with her free hand. "And don't call me *sugar*." She turned her body away from him and jerked on her arm again.

"Oh. Excuse me. I meant Special Agent *Sugar*." The wave of tenderness he felt was a complete surprise. But the wave of passion that pushed it aside with an erotic shove was nothing new. He'd been plagued by those sexy urges for most of this very long evening.

In one fell swoop, Marc swung her off her feet and into his arms. "Aw, the hell with it." He forgot his irritation and forgot the rules of decency along with it. "Let's just find out what's real and what's not—right now."

Four

"**M**arcus?" The look on Dana's face had to be pure amazement. Not so much because he'd physically assaulted her—they both knew she could've defended herself against him with little trouble.

No, she looked—self conscious. A bit frightened by her own lack of resistance, perhaps. Or maybe she was simply amazed because she'd let things get out of control. He wondered if she was feeling concerned by his actions…or if she felt as stunned by her own reactions as he did.

Lost in the sensual moment, Marc forgot everything as his blood heated and pulsed. He forgot about being arrested. He forgot she was an FBI agent. He surprisingly managed to even forget that he'd sworn off women forever.

"Dana." Desire roughened his voice as they stared into each other's eyes. He tried again. "Please…."

Never before had she heard anyone say her name in

quite that same raspy, pleading kind of voice. The sound sent licks of fire spiraling down her spine. She shivered in the flames, without really understanding why.

She would give anything to hear him say her name that way once more. But instinct made her afraid to ask for what she wanted. Afraid to break the spell. She wasn't frightened of him—only of herself.

A soft uncertain noise sounded in her ears, and she realized it came from her own throat. It surprised her, the same way she'd been amazed when she placed a hand against his chest to balance herself and found his heart beating as rapidly as her own.

Finding her throat suddenly dry, she swallowed hard. His eyes dropped to her mouth, and she knew in an instant what would come next. He lowered his head the few inches separating their mouths and grazed his lips against hers.

Soft. The thought registered with surprise. The texture of his mouth felt like velvet—so soft, so exotic.

Dana couldn't exactly remember when she'd last kissed a man—if she ever really had. But she did know for sure that it could not have been like this.

For all its gentleness, there was a deep demand in Marcus's kiss. Hunger and passion were buried under the guise of a tender touch. She was certain about his desires because the drugging insistence of them was pulling the same responses from her own body.

A breathless whimper rumbled deep and escaped her lips, amazing her yet again with such wanton responses to him. As if with a life of their own, her fingers began to knead the cotton of his shirt. The navy-blue pullover bunched as she flexed her hand.

She wished she had the nerve and the time to rip his

shirt all the way off so she could run her fingers through the hair on his chest. The vision of him shirtless was as clear to her now as it had been a few hours ago when he'd first stepped from his shower. And she felt every bit as desperate to touch that hair-covered flesh—to slide her palms over his work-hardened muscles...as she had then.

Marcus eased one of his hands away, slowly letting her slide down the full length of him, without ever breaking the kiss. She felt his stiffened flesh pressing against her belly, right through both their slacks.

When he tenderly placed his hands on her face and kneaded her jaw, she opened for him. His tongue caressed her lips, seducing its way past them to find her teeth. She opened wider yet and gingerly touched his tongue with hers.

Intoxicating and sweet. Like nothing she'd ever experienced before.

Marcus anchored a fist in her hair and slid the other hand down her back. Endlessly, his palm inched a heated path down her spine, finally coming to rest on her hip.

Deepening the kiss, he coaxed her tongue to wind around his. Then he drove deeper still, blasting her with a wicked heat. He dragged her hips tighter against his groin.

She melted against him. There was no resistance anywhere in her body. In her whole life she'd never felt so limp and needy. Wanting this, wanting him, she moaned into his mouth.

Marc heard the sound like a roar of white water across slickened rocks. She tasted sizzling hot, icy sweet. When he felt her hands tentatively touch his shoulders, it was as if the rest of the world simply ceased to exist.

Passion and power. He'd found all of that and more in her kiss. Feasting on her softness, he filled his hands with her rounded jeans-covered bottom.

He broke the kiss, needing to taste the rest of her. Licking his way up her jawline, he found her sensitive earlobe and suckled. What fascinating sensations she had stirred in him. He kissed his way down her neck, restlessly moving his hands up and down her sides, eager to fill his palms with her breasts.

Finally covering one breast with his hand, he lasered his mouth back across hers, letting the beast inside the man go free. He wanted to taste every inch. He wanted to go on, licking and lathing, until he could bury himself deep inside her welcoming body.

Somewhere, back in a still-rational part of his brain, he knew this was not how a man kissed a woman for the first time. But this was the kind of kiss—the kind of woman—that he'd dreamed about for all of his life.

Dana was so much more than anyone before. So strong, yet so tender. Passionate, vibrant and real. She was everything that Alicia had never been.

That shocking thought brought him up abruptly. The pain of remembering Alicia's betrayal threw ice water against his heated skin and numbed his desire. What in God's name was he doing?

Clutching lamely at Dana's shoulders, he levered himself away from her and tried to catch his breath. She reached out to him and opened her drugged eyes, silently pleading with him to come back.

Heaven knew that's what he wanted, too. He wanted to go on kissing her…and much more.

He shut his eyes and cursed through gritted teeth.

Dana found herself blinking furiously, but at last she cleared the confusion from her brain. "Where the hell did that come from, Danforth?" she demanded with a shaky voice. "What were you thinking?"

Marc opened his eyes wide, but took a step back. "I'm not sure. But whatever it was, you were thinking it too." The look in his eyes held the same accusations and disorientation that she was feeling.

Many inadequate images ripped through her, but she wasn't positive she could articulate any of them. She'd definitely wanted him to keep on kissing her. But the rational side of her knew it had been right for them to stop.

From deep in her gut, she tried putting up an invisible shield around her emotions. But her fingers wouldn't obey her brain and automatically went to her swollen lips, tentatively touching the still-pulsing flesh there.

It had never occurred to her that she might ever kiss a man like that. And for it to be *this* man—the man she was supposed to be using to get to the head of a dangerous cartel….

Well, she supposed there was just no explaining it. Not to him and certainly not to herself.

Clearing her throat, she pressed her lips together and tried to think. "Let's get inside the house before we're spotted," she finally managed. "Do the gates on your fence actually close and lock?"

Marc had been standing there, studying her in the glare of the automatic yard lights. "Yeah," he answered with a drawl. "At least they did a year ago when I first moved in. The chain-link is mostly just for Laddie, not for protection. But the dog has never needed fencing. Outside the house, he knows where he belongs."

"Go lock the gates then," she ordered. "I'll get a couple of things out of my trunk and meet you inside after I disarm the security system."

Her words seemed to shake him from his sensual stupor. "Make sure Laddie is inside the fence before I lock the gates," he told her before spinning around and heading off into the crisp autumn night.

After he'd gone, Dana finally took a huge deep, cleansing breath. She stood five foot eight and sometimes towered over men, but Marc's six-two had made him seem like a giant standing next to her.

Shaking the cobwebs from her head, she dug the duffel out of the trunk. Ridiculous. Men simply did not make her nervous. Never had. And she was determined that Marc Danforth would not be the first.

In all of her life…first in high school while walking the dangerous streets of her neighborhood, then in college taking law enforcement courses with tough ex-marines, and finally at Quantico during FBI training…she'd turned men into friends or enemies. But every single one of them had kept a respectful distance.

She'd never allowed any of them to push her, and she'd worked hard at being one of the guys. It had been important to her to maintain that professional distance.

Always managing to keep her sexual naiveté quite well-hidden, in high school and college it had been a matter of self-preservation. No dates meant no sex. No sex meant no chance of ending up with a scoundrel like her father.

Eventually, though, she'd stopped thinking about men as anything but friends, co-workers or suspects. And at this point in her life, it would be just too embarrassing to admit that she was inexperienced at something so basic as relations between men and women.

Dana threw the duffel over her shoulder and went to the back porch, calling Laddie as she went. Finding him standing on the step, eagerly awaiting her arrival, he made her smile.

"Good boy." Dana reached down and roughed-up the fur around his neck.

While disarming the alarm on the back of the house, she couldn't help wondering why she'd let Marc kiss her. Not only let him, but encouraged him.

When she opened the door, Laddie bolted around her and headed through the lighted kitchen into the darkness beyond. Nothing in the house seemed to be out of place. But because she trusted the dog to know when something was amiss, she instinctively touched the weapon holstered under her jacket.

Crossing through the kitchen and into the foyer, she flipped on the overhead lights. When she heard Marc unlocking and opening the front door, she headed toward the sound and motioned for him to come in quietly.

When he stepped into the glow of the house lights, the sight of him took the breath right out of her lungs. The man was one gorgeous hunk.

He was also extremely rich and quite the ladies' man, if grocery-store tabloids could be believed. The two of them were definitely not from the same universe, let alone in the same league.

Their kiss had been an aberration. A one-shot miscalculation. Nothing more. She vowed to keep her mind on business, and her eye on the goal of taking down Escalante.

"Stay where you are a minute," she whispered in her most professional tone of voice. "I want to check out the rest of the house."

He stopped, but his eyes sparkled with amusement. "Yes, ma'am. There's nothing wrong, is there?"

"Just checking. When I opened the door, the dog took off like he was chasing something." She flattened herself against the wall, drew her weapon and stealthily headed toward the bedrooms.

"Oh, no." Marc suddenly brushed past her down the hall and dashed through the first doorway on the right.

So much for him doing whatever she told him to do.

From her cursory inspection of this afternoon, she knew he'd turned into the guest room. "Marc, wait. Let me check…"

"No!" At his loud exclamation, Dana tensed.

Just as she reached the doorway, she heard him issuing commands. "Down, Laddie! Bad dog!"

"Do you need assistance?" It was pretty clear that Marc was okay. She couldn't vouch for the dog.

"We're fine," he called out.

Relaxing her shoulders, she moved further down the hallway, checking the other rooms. Everything was in place.

By the time she'd reholstered her Glock and returned to the guest bedroom, the dog was sitting on the floor at his master's feet with a terribly guilty expression in his sad eyes. "Did Laddie do something wrong?"

Marc shook his head. "He has a thing for this bed. No matter what I do to discipline him, he thinks the bed belongs to him. That's one of the reasons I try to keep him outside in his doghouse at night."

"Well, at least he doesn't sleep in *your* bed," she teased. "Wouldn't that be worse?"

Marc raised his chin and shot her a smoldering look. "If you don't keep the door to this room closed tonight, you'll find out. In fact, you may decide you'd rather bunk with me."

God, what had possessed her to talk about his bed? Judging from their one mind-blowing kiss, plenty of women had shared his bed. He was too good a kisser not to practice—a lot. She decided belatedly that she had to be the professional here and watch what she said.

But this whole relationship thing was beyond her experience. As an undercover agent, she had always carefully phrased every word—every gesture. She simply never sent unintended signals to the men she dealt with. Right from the beginning with Marc, however, she'd let too much of her true self out for him to see.

Well, no more.

So what if her heart pounded in her throat every time he looked at her? She was good at undercover work, wasn't she? From now on, she would just play the part of someone who didn't care that he had the power to tear her heart out with one touch of his lips.

"Let the dog stay inside," she told him. "We can use all the extra protection we can get.

"And you go on to bed now," she added casually. "I'll set the alarms. I'm a light sleeper, so you don't have to worry about anything. I'll handle it. Get a good night's sleep. You're going to need it."

He cocked his head and narrowed his eyes. "Right, sugar. I'm all for getting a good night's sleep."

Marc slowly walked toward her as she stood frozen in the doorway. The closer he came, the more she felt like running. But she stood her ground. In the next instant, however, he destroyed all her good intentions about remaining noncommittal.

Reaching over, he ran a finger lightly down the side of her cheek and then rubbed his thumb over her bottom lip. "But if you find Laddie too much of a handful…I'll keep a warm place for you in my. bed." He winked and grinned with a sexy twist of his lips. "Just in case."

Dropping his hand, he sauntered toward the master bedroom. But before rounding the corner, he turned his head to see if she was still glued in place watching his cute backside. Which she was.

He grinned one last time and disappeared into his room.

She was in big trouble.

Marc spent a couple of hours tossing and turning in his bed. He'd lost his edge with Dana. And after promising himself he wouldn't let another woman get under his skin.

But there was something about the woman that stirred his soul. Sighing, he tried pounding the pillow into submission for the eighteenth time and finally gave up.

After spending a sleepless night in jail, he'd been sure he would sleep like a rock in his own bed. But that was before a gorgeous woman with big, brown doe eyes moved in down the hall.

His traitorous body was not going to let him get any rest tonight. He rose and tugged on his robe, deciding to go to the kitchen. Maybe something warm in his stomach would help him relax.

When he opened the bedroom door, he noticed that it felt rather chilly in the rest of the house. Perhaps he should turn on the electric heat—or maybe build a fire in the fireplace.

October in Georgia could be deceiving. Days were usually hot and sticky. Leftover summer rains splashed down in puddles one minute that were sun-dried the next. But the nights could turn quite chilly. Last year they'd had frost on Halloween.

Creeping down the darkened hall, he passed by the partially opened door to the guest room. He guessed Dana had left the door open so she could hear what happened in the house during the night. A smirk lifted the corners of his mouth as he thought about her spending the night with Laddie sprawled out over that barely-room-for-one bed. She should've taken him up on the offer of spending the night in his bed. There would've been a lot more room.

It didn't take more than a moment for that image to register on his body. With her luscious body in the same bed, he was positive neither one of them would've gotten any sleep. Shoving those images into the recesses of his mind, he swallowed hard and tried not to think at all.

Marc went straight to the living room fireplace without turning on any lights. He opened the glass doors to the hearth and picked up an armload of precut pine logs from the wood box. After placing the logs on the grate, he set fire to the twigs he'd put under them.

He sat back on his heels in front of the hearth and used a poker to stir the kindling to flames. Concentrating on bringing the fire to life, he began to think about how he wanted to bring Dana's body to life. He would use just the right kindling touches and just the right firestormed kisses. With only one kiss, she'd proven that she was capable of becoming everyman's sexual fantasy. She'd been vibrant and erotic under his touch.

Lost in the memory of their sensual haze, Marc was jolted when the table lamp behind him switched on with a blinding glare. He nearly fell on his butt with surprise.

Instead, he caught himself and swiveled around to see what was going on. "What the hell…?"

Dana stood there, holding her gun loosely at her side. With the other hand, she kept a tight grip on Laddie's collar. "Couldn't sleep?"

Marc's heart was racing as the adrenaline of surprise churned through his veins. "No." He coughed and found his voice. "I didn't mean to frighten you. I was cold and wanted to light the fire."

Laddie lowered his head and made a distinctly unfriendly sound deep in his throat.

Dana let go of Laddie's collar and whispered something in his ear. The dog sat back on his haunches and his tongue lolled out of the corner of his mouth. He'd obviously found a new friend in the beautiful FBI agent. The big traitor.

"You didn't frighten me," Dana said quietly. "But Laddie insisted that we make sure you were all right."

She briefly checked the gun and placed it on the table beside her. "Is there anything I can do to help you sleep?"

Oh man. Was that a leading question.

He turned back to the fire before he slipped and told her exactly what he had in mind. "No, thanks. I was planning on making myself some hot coffee just as soon as I got the fire going." But at the moment, a good stiff shot of bourbon sounded like a better deal.

"Do you have any chocolate mix? I always think hot milk is better than coffee in the middle of the night."

"There's probably some in the pantry."

"Good. I'll go find it." She left the room and that bewitched devil dog, Laddie, trotted along at her heel.

A couple of lousy hours with Dana and man's best friend had turned on the hand that fed him. It wasn't the first time Marc had lost a best friend to a woman. But it still hurt. You'd think he would've learned a lesson the first time.

The fire snapped as the heat blazed against his hands and face. He replaced the poker and closed the glass doors, all the while thinking of how Dana had looked, standing there with his former best friend beside her.

She'd had on a gray sweatshirt that was a couple of sizes too big. The V-neck had slipped down one shoulder, revealing the curve of one of her creamy golden breasts. She obviously wore no bra underneath.

His hand flexed with the memory of how her breast had yielded to him earlier. A man could hardly forget so soon how sweet that felt. Or how he wished he'd had the opportunity to place his mouth around the jutting nipple. Or how…

When he looked down, he realized that the thin fabric of his pajamas and robe were revealing with crystal clarity every erotic thought he'd had. Damned biology.

Pulling the robe tighter, he straightened his shoulders and went off to find that bottle of bourbon.

As the first rays of sun changed the farmyard from pitch-dark of night into gray cast of dawn, Dana ran a comb through her shower-wet hair and slipped on her running shoes. At this hour, every muscle in her body yearned for a real run. But there would be no opportunity for that today. She couldn't leave Marc alone.

For a couple of hours last night, she'd sat at the kitchen table while he'd drunk himself into a sleepy fog. It was a good thing that over the years of being a covert agent she'd learned the art of listening. She'd let him tell her—for the third time—the history of what the cartel had done to his family. Then he told her every detail of how his time in jail had gone. Twice.

He'd been so miserable, feeling sorry for himself and trying not to recognize the sexual tension that they both knew flared between them. She'd been miserable too—not sure of what she wanted. One thing she was sure of; he was the cutest thing she'd ever seen.

She would be willing to bet the farm, though, that he'd be wishing for a total head transplant when he finally woke up this morning. Chuckling to herself, she finished dressing and slipped out of her room to go make the coffee. He was going to need it.

When she entered the kitchen, the smell of coffee brewing made her nerve endings itch. Nothing seemed out of place and she hadn't heard any kind of disturbance, so she quickly figured out it must've been Marc who had made the coffee. But where was he now?

Dana went to the outside door and found the alarm still set. But it could've easily been disarmed and reset, and there would be no clues. Checking the fine thread she'd placed across the threshold in case someone did get past the alarm system, she wasn't surprised to find it broken. Marc had gone outside. And after all her warnings about not going anywhere without her.

It finally hit her that Laddie was missing, as well. She'd ordered the dog to sit in the hall watching the master bedroom door while she'd been taking her shower.

She stepped onto the back porch and scanned the dreary horizon. After spotting Laddie moving noisily amongst the sheep, she relaxed her shoulders. But then she noticed Marc talking to an older man out near the barn, and the tension raced back through her hands and down her spine.

Dana watched as Marc shook the other man's hand, then turned and came toward her alone. The stranger walked away, heading in the direction of the far pasture out past the barn.

Dressed in jeans and a pecan-colored sweater that matched his eyes, Marc looked relaxed and devastatingly handsome for this hour of the morning. But he scowled at her when he came near. "You shouldn't be out here, Dana. Let's go back into the house."

She grimaced at his words. "You're a fine one to talk. Aren't you the one that shouldn't be outside, contacting strangers without me? I'm trained in defense, not you."

He grabbed her elbow and swung her around, still moving toward the kitchen door. "The man was my neighbor, William Stevens. I was arranging for him to take care of the animals for a few weeks. But now that he's seen you, he'll be wondering what's really going on. And I'd rather not be the subject of any more speculation if I can help it."

The stab of irritation hit her right between the tingling waves of pleasure at his touch. "Won't he simply believe I'm just another one of the many glamour girls you bring home? He wasn't close enough to get a good look."

Marc stopped at the bottom of the steps, released her and stood back to study her face. "Are you joking?" He answered his own question without waiting for her reply. "No, I can see you're not. What would make you say such a thing?"

"I've studied the background files on you, Danforth. There's a stack of newspaper clippings an inch thick, all with you cuddling, kissing or holding hands with various debutantes and models. Why wouldn't *everyone* just assume you bring them home?"

Marc checked the alarm system and found that she'd left it disarmed. "Inside." He spent a moment at the door waiting for her, then he must've realized he'd better try again. "We can talk about it if you'll come into the kitchen now. Please, Dana."

She swung around and scanned the horizon. "What about the dog?"

"Stevens said he'd take him to his farm for the time being. Laddie likes it over there with other dogs."

After they'd reentered the house, Marc poured coffee into two mugs and then sat at the table. Dana rearmed the alarm and joined him.

"Look," he began. "My family is well connected here in Savannah. For them, and because of my position at the firm, I have to attend an occasional charitable or political function. Sometimes I must escort a woman. But believe me, none of it is particularly fun…or personal."

Sipping her coffee slowly, she waited.

He looked thoughtful for a second then continued. "Except for one of my brothers and a cousin or two, I haven't brought anyone out here since I moved in."

Dana raised her eyebrows and pushed out her bottom lip. It wasn't that she doubted him—exactly. But it seemed hard to imagine.

"You don't believe me?" He stood and paced to the sink and back. "The truth is, I haven't had a real date in over a year. Ask anyone in my family. They'll tell you."

"I don't believe you'd lie, Marc." She finished her coffee and set the mug down on the table. "But it seems odd for a rich, good-looking man who is one of the town's most eligible bachelors to be celibate. What's the problem?"

Dana couldn't quite believe she'd made such a rude and nosy remark. On the other hand, she'd learned on the job that asking a surprise personal question could occasionally elicit a surprise honest answer.

Marc took both mugs to the sink and moved behind her chair. He leaned over to whisper, "Maybe I just need someone like you to inspire me. I'm sure you figured out last night that it's not a physical problem. There's no way you didn't feel the truth of that."

He came closer and nibbled on her earlobe. "Want to volunteer to be the first to break my abstinence?"

His voice gave her the shivers and his kiss sent heated bolts of sensual wanting through her body. She remembered quite well how hard his body had become when she'd plastered herself against it. The memory was burning gaps in her mind and causing other searing physical needs she hardly recognized. How could he turn a simple interrogation into something so sexy?

She stood and backed away, determined to wrest the upper hand back from him. "We're going to be working closely together for the next few weeks. I think we'd better not mention last night again. It was a mistake. It won't happen again."

He smiled at her, but didn't say a word. The silence sparked the air around them.

Dana cleared her throat and found her voice again. "You're just trying to make me forget the question." She took another step back. "So let me repeat, why haven't you been with a woman in over a year?"

Marc pressed his lips together. "I'm going to take a shower. We have a lot of plans to make today."

"Are you too chicken to answer me?"

"It's nothing, Dana. No big deal. I'll tell you all about it sometime when things get dull." He tugged his sweater over his head and headed for the master bedroom.

Left in the silence, she wondered if this assignment would end up being her worst nightmare. Not due to the cartel. Or because of the cocky, rich man's son she was forced to work with. But because of the way her body was bound and determined to betray her whenever Marc came near.

Five

He'd had just about all he could take. Marc spent a long grueling day, first watching Dana inspect the SUV, and then watching an FBI technician install bugging devices on his phones. It was so boring that he'd been nearly ecstatic when Uncle Harry called to invite them to Crofthaven for a family dinner meeting.

Normally, a summons to his father's home would've been depressing. But today he was grateful for the diversion.

If he hadn't had so many truly god-awful days in his lifetime, he would've been tempted to call this one the worst day of his life. As it was, the most he could say about today was that it was frustrating.

He wanted to do something to prove his innocence. And he needed to get moving—so he wouldn't be tempted to obsess over wanting Dana in his arms.

Her FBI boss had asked him to go about his business as usual until a plan to draw out Escalante could be developed. Marc's style would've been more along the lines of breaking into the cartel's den and beating the truth out of them. But he held back for Dana's sake, and managed to sit on his hands while she went about her job.

She was so competent and so obviously physically fit that the energy fairly rolled off her well-toned body in waves. He appreciated her intensity about the job and her professionalism—almost as much as he appreciated her lean physique. The more he drooled over her exquisite body while he watched her work, the more determined to keep his hands off of her he became.

Finally, Dana relented and agreed he could drive them over to Crofthaven in his SUV. Behind the wheel, he felt useful and a lot less ineffectual than he had all day.

"Do you go home often?" she asked as he drove them down the narrow highway. Her words were plain enough, but her smoky tones sent electric impulses through his veins and destroyed his resolve.

"Home? You mean Crofthaven?" He felt like a horny teenager whose hormones had turned him into an idiot.

He thought she must be nodding in the affirmative, but he'd decided against trying to catch a glimpse of her while he was driving. Keeping his mind off her body and his eyes on the road seemed like the best bet at the moment.

There were plenty of things for him to regret in his life. Causing an accident because he was ogling an FBI agent wouldn't be the best thing to add to the list.

"Uh… I don't exactly consider Crofthaven home,"

he said with a croak in his voice. "Actually, I doubt that any of my siblings do, either."

"But weren't you raised there? I thought I read that in your file?"

"We had rooms in the house. There's a world of difference between that and thinking of someplace as home."

He turned off the highway and headed down the country road that meandered along the Atlantic coast. "I suppose when I was very small and my mother and grandparents were still alive, I thought of Crofthaven as a wonderful home. The grounds are extensive, there's a private beach and lots of places for a kid to play. But all that changed after Dad came back from Vietnam and then Mother died in a car crash."

"How old were you when your mother died?"

"Almost five."

"That must've been hard on all of you."

Marc heard the sympathy in her voice. "It was a long time ago, Dana. Dad hired nannies and then packed us all up and sent us to boarding schools. On holidays and vacations we spent most of our time at Uncle Harry and Aunt Miranda's house, downtown in Savannah's historic district. If I thought of anywhere except the farm as home now, it would have to be their house."

As he drove the SUV closer to the Crofthaven gates, Marc began to notice cars parked along the sides of the roadway. Odd. It looked almost as if someone was holding a big party and more cars had shown up than the parking lot would hold. But that could never happen on a place as vast as Crofthaven.

When he finally realized what was going on, it was

nearly too late to do anything about it. "Oh, hell! The local tabloids have arrived. Scrunch down in your seat, Dana." He stepped on the gas pedal. "I know a secret entrance that the gardeners use. I'll blow past the reporters and double back. But in case they recognize my SUV, you probably don't want to be seen with me."

Her quick shift in position was nearly automatic. "This wouldn't be a problem if you'd let me drive," she ground out through gritted teeth from her spot under the dash. Less than thirty seconds later, the SUV slowed. "Are we past them?"

"Yeah. I don't think they noticed us at all." Marc took a left and she sat back up in the seat. "The gardener's gate is on a combination lock. I'll have to get out to open it." He pulled in between two rows of dense shrubs and stopped.

"Leave the car running and the door open," she ordered before he jumped out.

While he was gone, she dug around in her backpack for the FBI-issued SAT phone. Connecting immediately to the special task force that her boss had set up to assist in the investigation and apprehension of Escalante, Dana barked out a few questions. The special agent who answered said he would get back to her.

Marc slid back behind the wheel and drove through the gate. "I don't think any of the reporters noticed us." Once through, he slowed the SUV. "I have to relock the gate."

"I'll do it." Dana was out of the SUV in an instant. Undercover operatives usually didn't have to fight off the glare of the tabloids to do their jobs. How in the world was she going to get through this mission?

"What do you suppose those reporters wanted?" she asked when she returned to the car.

Marc shrugged as he wound the car down a tiny tree-covered lane. "They're probably waiting for Dad. He's running for the Senate seat, you know."

"Those guys looked like they were hot on the trail of a scandal. I have my doubts that they're the standard political-beat reporters."

After they'd driven a quarter of a mile up the private lane, she glanced around at the lush landscaping. The green lawn was manicured and trimmed. In the distance, the paved drive that led from the wrought-iron front gates to the main house could be seen, outlined by magnificent oak trees that were covered over by low-hanging mosses. The place looked like a picture post-card of the old South.

Only bigger and richer.

They topped a little crest and were surrounded by an orchard and the flower gardens beyond. The main house stretched out as far as she could see, and seemed to consist of three floors with at least two wings. To Dana's mind, this place could only be called a mansion. Or maybe she would call it a fairy-tale castle.

Marc drove past gardening sheds and ended up in front of a ten-car garage located behind the mansion. "Hope you don't mind if we go through the kitchen," he said. "I don't want to take a chance on running into any of Dad's political buddies. They usually meet in one of the front rooms this late in the afternoon."

"Kitchen's fine with me."

By the time they walked through an enclosed porch and then a series of mudrooms, Dana was nearly lost.

The place was enormous, and the kitchen was big enough to feed a hundred people. With its professional-looking equipment, she was positive it was set up better than most restaurants.

Marc introduced her to the family's cook, Florence, as they made their way to a swinging door on the other side of the big kitchen. "Where is everyone, Flo?" he asked.

Before the cook could answer, a paunchy man in his early fifties came through the door. "There you are." He shook Marc's hand and beamed at him from under his stock of thick dark hair and bushy eyebrows. "How are you holding up, son? You look tired."

"I'm all right, Uncle Harry. But I'll be a lot better when I find the proof to clear my name." Marc turned to her. "Dana, I'd like for you to meet my uncle, Harold Danforth."

The older man turned his kind blue eyes in her direction. "Ah yes. The FBI agent who's going to help clear Marc's name." He took her hand. "I've heard you are quite capable. Thank you for taking an interest in my nephew. We've all been very worried about him."

"Where's Dad?" Marc asked his uncle.

"He and Nicola and Jake are in a last minute campaign strategy meeting in the library."

Marc lowered his voice to a whisper. "What's with all the reporters outside?"

"Nicola's best guess is that John Van Gelder's campaign forces have been spreading rumors that Abraham will be calling a press conference to announce he's bowing out of the race."

"What?" Marc asked with force. "But why? There's hardly a month left until the election."

Harold looked thoughtful. "I believe its supposed to be due to your arrest. The rumor mill apparently has it that Abraham is so embarrassed by your *arrest* that he doesn't want the taint of your *crimes* to rub off on his good name." He screwed up his mouth in a scowl. "Humph. As if there'd never been a Senator tainted by family scandals…or by their own personal crimes…for that matter."

"Well, it's just…ridiculous," Marc sputtered.

He was about to say more, but his uncle laid a firm hand on his shoulder. "Don't give it another thought, Marc. Of course it's ridiculous. Your father has no intention of quitting. Abraham never quit anything intentionally in his whole life."

Harold smiled up at his nephew, who stood a good four inches taller. "Your father knows you're innocent of the charges, and it's only a matter of time until that's proven. We *all* know you're innocent, Marc. And we want to help."

Dana was stunned by the tender look she saw in Harold Danforth's eyes when he spoke to Marc. She'd seen it twice before coming from the Danforths. Those times it had been coming from his brothers, Adam and Ian. And now that same loving look came from his uncle.

The obvious affection gave her a knot in the center of her stomach. Family. Oh, what she would've given when she was a child to feel anything resembling that tenderness from her own family.

Not only was Marc a world away from her by reason of his wealth and privilege. But he was also in a different universe when it came to knowing about family trust and honor. She stifled a sigh, quickly deciding that the two of them had nothing on which to build a relationship.

All those little tingles of connection to him she'd been feeling must've been coming from her imagination. Or perhaps…it had just been the lust talking. She'd never wanted a man so badly. Her body apparently was confusing desire with caring.

Well, it was time to go back to her job. No more daydreaming about someone who was on the other side of such a great divide.

"I'm on my way to find your aunt Miranda. We'll be going out to the terrace in a minute to visit with our new daughter-in-law and grandson," Harold told Dana with a smile. "Jake will be joining us shortly for dinner. He's very anxious to put his two cents' worth into any plan that will come to Marc's defense." Harold headed back inside the house.

Marc touched her elbow and led her out the way they'd come.

"Who's Jake?" she whispered.

"Harry and Miranda's son, Jacob Danforth," he said under his breath. "He and Adam are the founders of the D & D Coffeehouse chain. Jake and his new wife have been helping with Dad's campaign during the last couple of months, while most of the rest of us have been tied up with other things. Jake's an absolute genius when it comes to PR and raising money."

Dana followed Marc out into shadowy sunshine that was flooding the parklike grounds with golden stripes from a beautiful fall sunset. It was a good thing she had instant memory recall. Just keeping track of all the family members was a chore not many could handle.

* * *

"Marc!" Jake's son, Peter, spotted them the minute they stepped onto the terrace.

The little boy threw down his toys and raced across the lawn toward them. Marc knelt on one knee and braced himself, spreading his arms out wide. Peter's chubby little legs churned furiously as the boy shrieked and giggled, running full out. It was a game the two of them had played for several months now, ever since Jake had discovered that he had a son and married Larissa, Peter's mom.

Peter reached the terrace and flung himself into Marc's open embrace, knocking both of them over. Marc laughed so hard he barely had the breath left to capture the squirming child against his chest, protecting him from the hard surface as they rolled over.

"Peter, stop that. You're ruining Marc's clothes." Larissa came running toward the terrace, trying to keep a straight face. But it was a losing battle.

Finally, Marc wrestled Peter around and managed to balance them both as he got to his feet. "Okay, partner," he said to the giggling little boy. "That's enough now. There's someone I want you to meet."

Dana eyes were wide and glittering with fun as she watched Peter squirm. Marc dusted the boy off, straightened his T-shirt and hiked up his pants. With every touch, Peter giggled and stomped his feet with laughter.

Marc's heart skipped wildly with affection for the sweet child. For the first time since he'd lost himself in Dana's kiss last night, Marc completely forgot about being arrested and framed by the cartel. Nothing could be very wrong in this world as long as children could laugh so freely.

He threw his arm around Peter to keep him still and introduced the boy to Dana. She bent over and extended her hand. "How do you do, Peter?"

"I'm four," he told her.

Out of breath, Larissa came up on the terrace and swung Peter into her arms. "When someone says 'how do you do,' you're supposed to answer 'fine thank you'." She looked as if she was still trying to keep the smile off her face, but her eyes were giggling like a schoolgirl's.

Marc introduced Dana to Larissa and they made their way over to the huge glass-top table that had been set for dinner. He went past the table and checked the bar for ice, offering both women a drink.

"You two fix yourselves something," Larissa told them. "I'm going to take Peter inside and clean him up for dinner." She carried her son off through the French doors. But long after Marc lost sight of the boy, he could still hear Peter chatting on about the meaning of *fine*.

"Cute kid," Dana chuckled.

"Yeah, he's the best. He's the kind that makes me wish I had a few dozen of my own."

Dana looked startled for a minute, then she laughed. "Good luck finding a woman that'll agree to be the mother to such a brood."

Chuckling along with her, he offered her a drink, but she shook her head. "I'd better keep my mind clear so I can tell one of you family members from the next."

Just then Jake appeared at the kitchen door. But before Marc could introduce his cousin to Dana, she had to excuse herself to take a cell phone call.

Jake looked after her as she strolled down the garden path talking into the phone. "Didn't hear the phone buzz, did you? She must've had it on silent ring." He turned back to Marc. "She's the FBI agent Ian's been telling us about, isn't she?"

"Yeah. And she's really something, Jake. Wait until you talk to her." Marc couldn't seem to take his eyes off of Dana's retreating backside. The way her jeans cupped that rounded bottom and the way she swung her hips when she walked were driving crazy images through his mind.

Jake slapped him on the back and brought his attention back to the moment. "It's easy to see what *you* think of her. But you need to keep your mind on getting out of this mess with the cartel."

Marc turned around to his cousin and narrowed his eyes. "What's happening with the campaign?"

Jake shook his head. "We're trying to keep it on track. Nicola has planned a final statewide campaign swing. We leave tomorrow for a couple of weeks' worth of whistle-stops throughout the state."

"Dad's still running ahead in the polls, isn't he?"

"By a wide margin. We've been trying to convince him to use your arrest to make a statement about family and privacy. But he's reluctant to bring it up with the press."

Marc wasn't entirely positive the word "reluctant" could ever be applied to his father. He'd always imagined that Abraham Danforth made use of every opportunity to discuss his viewpoints with the public. But before he could ask anything else, the terrace was suddenly bustling with activity.

Larissa came back outside with Peter. Uncle Harry and Aunt Miranda, followed by his father and Nicola, made their entrances through the patio doors. And Dana walked back up the path, stuffing the phone into her backpack. At the same moment, Florence stepped out of the kitchen door and told him that dinner was ready and they would be serving it outside shortly, if everyone could take their seats.

Marc introduced Dana to his assembled family members and to Nicola Granville, his father's campaign aide. After a rather boisterous dinner, Aunt Miranda took Peter inside for his bath. Miranda was absolutely wild about her newly discovered grandson, and Marc had to agree that the kid was really something.

The rest of the adults stayed seated around the cleared dinner table, drinking coffee and talking about Marc's predicament with the cartel.

His father had been rather silent throughout the dinner. But Marc was never entirely sure what his dad was thinking about things. The two of them hadn't been exactly close over the years. Their relationship was more like a superior officer to a raw recruit. Marc supposed it was do to his father's many years as a Navy SEAL.

"Marc," his father began from the other end of the table. "Tell me what the FBI plans for you."

"I think it would be better if Dana told us, Dad."

Dana was sitting next to him and had been particularly quiet throughout the meal. Now she looked up at the assembled group and smiled.

"My superior, Special Agent in Charge Steve Simon, is completing plans for us. His goal, of course, is ultimately to capture Ernesto Escalante. While he formulates his overall plan, Marc and I are to try to find a way into the cartel to discover a direct link to Escalante. That means—"

"Excuse me, young lady." Abraham Danforth interrupted Dana with his firm voice and commanding presence. "I'm glad the FBI wants to remove Escalante from the U.S. drug scene. And I know his capture would not only take the strain off my family but would be a great bonus for the FBI. What I want to know is what assistance my son, Marc, can expect from the FBI in return for his help."

Dana looked only slightly taken aback by such a direct assault from a man who, in a few short months, would likely be sitting on the Senate committee that oversees the Treasury Department and the FBI.

"We will agree to turn over all of our unclassified findings to his attorney to help with his defense," she replied.

Abraham slowly shook his head, frowning deeply at her. "Not good enough. I want total immunity for Marc. I want all the charges dropped…or none of the family will share any information with the FBI."

"Dad…" Marc was stunned. What his father was asking was only fair, he supposed. But it might be much more than the FBI was willing to give. All Marc wanted was a chance to prove he was innocent.

Abraham ignored Marc's interruption and continued to stare at Dana. "And…I want an absolute guarantee of his safety. Are you willing to personally make that guarantee?"

Dana surreptitiously straightened her spine and raised

her chin to face Abraham Danforth square on. Marc thought she was the most spectacular woman he'd ever met.

"I can promise Marc…and his family…that I'll protect his life with my own. However, his complete safety will be partially his own responsibility. He must do exactly as he is told, or the FBI cannot promise anything." She stopped and took a breath. "As for total immunity…I will put your request through the proper channels."

Abraham steepled his fingers in front of his face. "I expect that you will." He turned to face Marc. "Are you willing to temporarily go along with the FBI's plans without having their assurances on your ultimate deal?"

"Yes. I'm more than willing," he truthfully told his father. "I have to do something, Dad. I can't just sit around and let other people decide my fate."

His father smiled at him—one of Abraham's very rare smiles. It was so unusual to see the man with anything but a fierce expression on his face, that the whole table was speechless.

Everyone but Nicola. "Please tell us your immediate plans, Dana. We've been arranging a statewide campaign swing but perhaps we should stay in town to help Marc."

Dana relaxed her shoulders. "I talked to my boss right before dinner, and he is still convinced that for the time being Marc and his family should go about their business as if nothing unusual has happened. SAC Simon thinks the cartel will be more likely to contact either Marc or Ian if they think things appear normal.

"Apparently Marc's brother, Ian, is willing to have

him pretend to come into work everyday," she continued. "As long as I'm there to give him protection."

Dana hesitated for a second in order to give everyone time to absorb that information. "We'll be using some of the Danforth office space to set up our investigation. But…" She hesitated yet again. "The biggest problem with the scheme will be the tabloid reporters. I haven't had a chance to speak to Marc about this, but he's going to have to find a good excuse for why I'll be with him at all times and…make it seem normal."

"You could be his new administrative assistant," Jake offered.

"No," Larissa contradicted her husband. "That's no good. They could be seen together anytime, twenty-four hours a day. The gossip would begin immediately."

"Well, speaking from an image standpoint, your best defense is a good offense," Nicola said softly. "Marc and Dana will have to appear to be lovers, about to be engaged, and so much in love they can't leave each other's side… even for the work day.

"I'll schedule a press briefing for first thing in the morning," Nicola offered. "The tabloids have been trying to find out what Abraham thinks of Marc's arrest. A good way to deflect it will be if he begins by declaring his son's innocence and then goes on to announce Marc's engagement. That'll change the focus for a while."

Dana had been afraid someone was going to come up with that solution. There was no way she could ever pass as someone Marc would marry. She didn't belong to the same social circle. Not even close.

"But…I'm…not prepared to do that kind of undercover operation. I don't have the right clothes or...the right training. How in the world are we going to convince the paparazzi?"

Everyone at the table smiled at her, but it was Larissa who made the most sense. "I can tell you from personal experience that the tabloids aren't strictly interested in the truth—as long as it makes a good story."

Larissa swiveled around to take her new husband's hand in her own. "But we just happen to have someone in our extended family who's an expert in 'scandal' journalism ...not that she's personally into that kind of thing."

Jake smiled at his new bride. "Of course." He turned to Marc. "I'll bet Jasmine will be willing to help you with the tabloids. You might want to check with her on the information she's accumulated about the cartel, too. Wes tells me her files on them are quite extensive."

Marc stuck his forehead with the palm of his hand. "Jasmine," he began. "I should've already thought to ask her about the cartel. I'll give her a call tonight."

"Who's Jasmine?" Dana asked.

"Jasmine Carmody Brooks," Jake told her. "She recently married Wesley Brooks, my old roommate and my partner in the D & D Coffeehouse chain. It's a long story. Get Marc to fill you in."

"And about getting you prepared for this *operation*," Nicola said, with a smile in her eyes. "Image consulting is my job. I'll give you a short lesson this evening."

She tilted her head and studied Dana, then turned to question Jake. "Do you know if your sister, Imogene, could break away from that gorgeous new husband of her's tonight? She's forgotten more about clothes and makeup than most women will ever know."

Dana's head was spinning. The names of family members were running around in her brain. And the idea of being anyone's fiancée, even just for pretend, was making her sweat.

Then Marc reached under the table and squeezed her hand, and everything changed.

Six

On the way back to his farm, Marc wasn't sure of what to say to her. He'd wanted to apologize for subjecting her to his family, particularly his father. But on the other hand, this kind of thing was probably in Dana's job description.

Anyway, not knowing what to say kept him quiet on the long drive home. Dana seemed to be off in her own world, and the silence between them apparently didn't bother her at all.

Tomorrow morning, during Abraham's press conference, the papers would be notified of their upcoming marriage. The idea was to make the cartel believe he was so unconcerned about his arrest that he'd chosen this time to become engaged.

One possible outcome would be for Escalante to believe the ruse and start pushing Marc and Ian all the harder. Another possibility was Escalante would not believe it, and instead would believe that Marc was running scared—hopefully leading the cartel into thinking that they had the upper hand and should relax their guard.

Either way, the cartel might make a mistake. That looked like his best shot at the moment. But a pretend engagement, especially to someone as spectacular as Dana, left Marc depressed and shaken. His last engagement turned out to be such a monumental disaster that the very mention of it embarrassed him no end.

When he drove up to the chain-link fence surrounding his farm and stopped, Marc glanced quickly over to the sexy FBI agent who was about to become his pretend fiancée. "I'll get the gate."

"No," Dana snapped back. "Don't exit the vehicle until I can cover you. I'll take care of the gate. Drive on through when it's open and I'll lock up."

A few minutes later they were dragging the mountain of clothes and boxes of makeup that Imogene had lent to Dana out of the back of the SUV. "Jeez," he said as he hefted one of the boxes into the house. You're too beautiful to need makeup at all. What's all this junk for, anyway?"

She didn't answer him until they were safely inside. "I need it for…" she stuttered, then stopped and stared at him. "Do you really think I'm beautiful?"

"Sure." It took a minute for her question to register as he helped her hang the clothes in the guest closet. Didn't she realize how truly gorgeous she was?

"Dana, hold on a minute." Taking her hand, he made her stop unpacking clothes and focus on his face.

"You're a very unique woman, Special Agent Aldrich. There aren't many as strong, competent and intelligent at their jobs as you are. But…you're so much more. You can also be soft and gentle when needed. You light up any room just by your presence. And…you are one of the sexiest women I've ever met."

As he ran a finger across her cheek, her eyes opened to the size of two full moons. Marc tried to find the words to make her see herself as he saw her. "Your big brown eyes hold every mystery ever kept by womankind. Your skin is pure pleasure to touch. And your hair…"

He grabbed a handful of her deep ebony ringlets and totally lost his train of thought. Leaning toward her, he hovered between agony and ecstasy. All he could see was her pale soft lips, just inches from his own. But he wasn't sure she wanted the same thing.

Close enough to smell a slight scent of musk, he bent forward and pressed his lips to hers. She whimpered with an erotic sound that fired his blood. She was all woman now.

Marc deepened the kiss, needing to consume her before the ground gave way under his feet. "I want you," he whispered into her mouth.

Suddenly, he felt an angry shove against his mid-section. Slightly dazed, he lifted his head and gazed down into her face.

"Nice try, counselor." She grinned as she stepped away from him. "That's quite a line you've got going there. But I told you last night that sharing kisses is a mistake. I'm here to protect you and find evidence against the cartel. If we can locate Escalante, all the better. I'm not here to jump into your bed."

She walked over to the bedroom door and held it open, indicating she was ready for him to leave. "It's late. We'll be going to your office in the morning, just as you usually would. You'd better get some rest."

Reluctantly, he shuffled out the door. But before she could close it against him, he turned back.

"The heat is there between us, sugar," he told her. "You can't make it go away just because you don't want it. Sooner or later that heat will bubble over. Neither of us can stop it."

She laughed and raised her eyebrows. "I have a lot more control than that…sugar. Now go to bed. I'll keep an eye on things tonight. You get a good night's sleep."

He pressed his lips together and stepped back enough so that she could close the door in his face. Lord, this was going to be a tough night.

Muttering under his breath, Marc went down the hall and prepared himself for bed—alone. But he was absolutely positive he wasn't going to get a wink of sleep.

He was a brilliant corporate attorney. That's what everyone told Dana the next morning at the Danforth offices. Everyone said so, including Marc's secretary and all three of his junior assistants, two of whom were women.

But none of the women in the place had so much as hinted that Marc ever made a move on them. And Dana definitely tried to leave the way open for them to share the gossip. She wasn't sure how knowing about his private life would help her with the job, but she still wanted to know.

At the office she felt totally out of her comfort zone,

dressed in the black Donna Karan suit and designer high heels that Imogene had made her promise to wear. However, she didn't seem to be out of place there. A few of the women complimented her on the suit, but they were all dressed very much the same way.

By mid-afternoon, her feet were killing her and she was beginning to believe that Marc Danforth was a saint. She sat down in the conference room he'd taken over for their use. Kicking off her shoes under the table and rubbing her nylon-clad feet together, Dana figured the man had better be everything he'd claimed to be. Otherwise, she would be forced to kill him when this was all over—if for no other reason than she'd actually had to put on these crazy high heels for him.

She couldn't wait for the work day to be done so she could get back into her jeans and running shoes. But in the meantime, she worked on setting up the computer Marc's secretary had provided. Dana entered her password into the Bureau's covert Web site and was immediately allowed into the FBI files they'd begun compiling on the cartel.

"Hi. How's it going?" Marc sauntered in a little while later, followed by a very sophisticated dark-skinned woman dressed in a soft aqua pants suit. "Dana, I want you to meet Jasmine Carmody Brooks. She's brought us her files on the cartel."

Dana took Jasmine's outstretched hand and the two of them immediately understood each other. By her firm no-nonsense handshake and the clearly determined look in her big brown eyes, Dana knew Jasmine was just as much of a competitive go-getter as she was.

Jasmine seemed to be sizing her up, as well. "There'll

be a small article in tomorrow's paper, announcing Marc's engagement to the daughter of one of Abraham's old navy buddies from Louisiana—a Miss Dana Delecroix. I spoke to your superior, Steve Simon, and he said he'd fix it so that you had a background there in case anyone checked.

"Abraham mentioned the happy news this morning at his press conference when someone questioned him on Marc's arrest," Jasmine continued with a smile. "It proved to be quite a diversion."

Marc pulled out a chair at the conference table for her. They all sat down while Jasmine unearthed a stack of files from a leather briefcase and placed them on the table.

"Dana, Jasmine tells me that a couple of tabloid reporters are sneaking around downstairs, trying to get a line on where we are and when they can try for a picture," Marc said with a grin. "Are you going to be ready for your first run-in with the paparazzi when we leave here later?"

Dana felt herself grimace and tried to change it into a casual smile. "You sure we can't just give them the slip? I guarantee you I'm better at hiding than they are at finding people."

Marc chuckled, but shook his head. "Sorry. But they'll be bored soon enough, once we let them have what they want. Tomorrow someone else will be their target."

"Okay, fine," she muttered. Turning to Jasmine, she watched her place the manila folders on the table.

"I started collecting information on the coffee suppliers and the cartel back in April, right after the Danforth warehouse office explosion," Jasmine said as she flipped through the files. "Ian has seen all this information. But I told him I wouldn't break the story while Marc was still involved."

"Good thing," Dana told her. "I suspect that Marc is only alive now because he's the pawn the cartel is using to get to Ian. You break the story on the cartel and Marc's usefulness is over."

Once the words were out of her mouth, Dana had a queasy feeling deep in the pit of her stomach. She snuck a peek at Marc's guarded expression.

Marc. Bright, energetic and a spectacular kisser, Marc Danforth. She couldn't imagine him being killed, or that anyone could take his fantastic life away from him.

Dana swallowed hard and narrowed her eyes on the folder in Jasmine's hand.

"These are pictures that I've been taking of people coming and going from the coffee suppliers' offices over on Montgomery Street," Jasmine told them. "I can identify some of the men, but there are a few that I can't place."

Dana looked over her shoulder as Jasmine spread the photos out before her. "There must be hundreds of pictures here." She looked at each one as Jasmine handed them over. "And the quality is terrific."

Dana studied each shot carefully. "Wow. Great telephoto lens work here, Jasmine. And just look at the infrared quality of these." She passed each picture to Marc, after checking the backs for dating references.

"At the beginning I thought I'd get a few candid shots that would be useful for an article," Jasmine said. "But the longer I sat there, the more I realized that nothing much happened at that office during the daylight hours. No one important went in or out. So I started watching the building late at night. That's when I got the best shots."

"What did Wes have to say about all this late night work?" Marc asked.

"You know Wes. He's a computer fanatic," Jasmine told Dana with a chuckle. "After-midnight work might as well be broad daylight to him."

Jasmine hesitated a moment before continuing. "Well that is, until he suddenly figured out which part of town I'd been going to all those late nights. He has asked me not to go back alone."

Dana shot a concerned glance toward the self-assured woman. "He's absolutely right. Don't go there alone…in fact…don't go back there at all. Let the FBI take over the surveillance now."

Jasmine raised her chin. "It's my story."

"Naturally. I'll ask my boss to make sure you're the one to break any news." Dana spotted a blurry face in one of the night shots. "Is that Escalante?"

"I'm not sure. I've only seen his photo on the Internet." Jasmine handed her a magnifying glass. "Whoever that man is, he arrived in the company of several goons and a chauffeur. It could be Escalante."

Marc remained quiet as they rifled through the photos. The idea that he was looking at drug lords—at men who held his fate in the palm of their hands—had taken the spark right out of him.

He glanced down at the picture in his hand and almost passed it by. Then the reality of what he was seeing hit him. "I can't believe this. Jasmine, have you ever seen this man before?" Waving the picture at her, he forced himself to calm down and try to hold the photo steady.

Both women looked at it. "Actually, that man did look familiar to me," Jasmine replied after she'd checked the photo in his hand. "But I haven't been able to place him. I do remember that he showed up at the coffee suppliers office just before dawn twice in the last month."

The anger swiftly blasted past his normal reserve. "Son of a bitch." Marc handed the picture to Dana. "This is David Chastain. He's an assistant federal prosecutor for our district. And he's in charge of prosecuting my case."

"Well, that makes him a very interesting man in my book," Dana said calmly.

"Interesting?" He tried to keep his voice steady but tiny cracks of tension burst through. "Don't you see what this means? Chastain must be working for the cartel. He's the one that helped them frame me."

"Again," Dana began. "Interesting premise. But you don't have any proof."

"Proof? Why else would a federal prosecutor be sneaking into a known cartel front? And before dawn at that?"

Dana laid her hand on his forearm. "Calm down, Danforth. We'll run a background check on him. That'll give us a start. Then we'll check his bank records and credit lines."

He knew she was just trying to placate him. "All of that is circumstantial," he ground out. "And besides, it'll take too long. You heard Ian. We've only got a couple more weeks to get my name cleared or Ian gives in to the cartel."

"We can't panic here and ruin the investigation," she said softly. "Let's just take each step as it comes. We'll find the proof we need to clear your name."

Marc muttered to himself, knowing it was useless to argue with her. But he would be damned if any fresh-faced prosecutor was going to get away with bringing down the Danforth family. He would just have to think of something.

Dana made arrangements with Jasmine to copy all of her notes to turn over to the FBI. Then she wrote her a receipt for the photos. Meanwhile, Marc stood up and paced the room, trying to come up with a plan.

"Jasmine," Dana said at last. "Something just occurred to me. Where were you when you took these pictures? In a vehicle on the street?"

Jasmine shook her head. "No. I considered that. But I came to the conclusion that I'd be too exposed."

"Good thinking. So where were you?"

"The newspaper just happens to own one of the warehouses across the street from the cartel's office," Jasmine told her through a grin. "They store newsprint and extra equipment there. It was actually quite comfortable too…except for an occasional rat."

"Hmm. Do you think you could get me a key to the place? Without giving away who wants it, that is?"

Jasmine shrugged a shoulder. "Probably. I can try."

The afternoon was nearly gone, and Marc didn't want to hang around the office any longer. So he thanked Jasmine for all her help and told Dana to get ready to face the reporters downstairs.

On their way down in the elevator, he could feel her trembling beside him. "Just don't say anything to any of them, slick," he murmured. "You'll be a big hit if you simply stand there and smile. The cameras will love that face of yours." He took her hand and squeezed it to give her a little bit of his own strength.

"Smiling will be the hardest part," she told him. But he also noticed that she straightened her shoulders and lifted her chin with a determined grimace.

As it turned out, there were only a handful of reporters hanging around by the employee entrance. Most of them seemed to be photographers and not terribly interested in getting long quotes.

"When are you two planning on tying the knot?" one of them yelled out, amid the click of shutter lenses.

"As soon as we can," Marc replied with a casual air.

"Aren't you afraid the nuptials might have to be held in the slammer?" someone else asked.

Before he could answer that one, Dana turned to the man with a wide smile. "Not at all. In this country, innocent people don't go to jail for crimes they didn't commit."

That got a huge laugh from the crowd, and the flashbulbs popped around them frantically. He bent over to whisper in her ear. "Nice save, sugar. Thanks."

After twenty more minutes of nonstop smiling, Marc thanked everyone and helped Dana into the passenger side of the SUV. He drove away slowly, watching the reporters disperse in his rearview mirror.

"I imagine that ought to hold them," he told her.

"I hope so. I think my face is permanently stuck in this position." She rubbed her cheeks with her palms.

"How about if we go home and I fix us a little something to eat? I'll give you a back rub after dinner—as a reward for a great save with the paparazzi."

She shot him a sideways scowl, but then reached down and slipped off her shoes. "Make it a foot rub and you're on. But first, drive around town a little. We need to deliver these files to the FBI office and make sure no one is following us."

The normal twenty-minute drive home took over an hour. And Marc spent most of it racking his brain for a plan to link David Chastain to the cartel and save his skin.

Finally, he decided that he wanted to break into Chastain's office and rummage through his files. Maybe with a little luck he'd find incriminating evidence. Looking over to Dana, Marc came to the conclusion that she would never agree to such a thing. It was totally illegal—and possibly dangerous.

So now he had to dream up a way to get out of the house without her.

Treating her like a queen, with a steak dinner, a bottle of his best merlot and a long soaking bath, was more his pleasure than hers. By midnight, sitting in front of the fireplace, she was groggy and pliable. Just the way he'd hoped she would be by now.

Stretching his arms, he gave a good imitation of a yawn. "Guess it's time to hit the sack." He stood and turned to her.

"Mmm, hmm," she groaned. "It's been a nice evening, Marc. Thank you."

He pulled her to her feet. But she came up like a rag doll and ended pressed into his chest. Having her there, cuddled against him all soft and warm, made the whole scene much too intimate and cozy. He considered dragging her off to his bed instead of putting her into hers and then sneaking off for his breaking-and-entering caper.

She was nearly asleep standing up, and Marc shook his head at his own foolishness. Naw. Dana had made it clear enough that her first allegiance was to the law and the FBI. He wouldn't take advantage of her in a moment of weakness. Hers or his.

"Let's get you to bed, sugar," he mumbled. What he'd decided to take advantage of was the opportunity to prove his innocence.

Marc lifted her off her feet and swung her into the guest bed. "Night, Dana. Sleep tight." He paused only long enough to pull the blankets around her and to smooth away a soft curl that covered her cheek.

Creeping down the hall to his bedroom, he figured he would give her a half hour to fall sound asleep. His plan was going to be tricky. She'd already proven she was a light sleeper. But without Laddie around, Marc knew he could get out of the house without waking her.

He turned on the TV in his bedroom. Though he never watched the thing, the noise would make a great cover. Then he turned off all the lights and waited.

When he was nearly sleepy enough to decide to give up the whole idea, Marc knew it was now or never. He slipped down the hall past her closed bedroom door and snuck into the darkened kitchen. He planned to go out the back door and then idle the car out of the yard.

With his shoes in hand, Marc made it to the door. But right before he put his hand on the alarm to disable it, the image entered his mind of doing this exact same thing as a teenager at boarding school. What was the matter with him? A grown man, sneaking out of his own house.

Dana. She'd be so upset when she discovered he'd gone off without her. He couldn't stand imagining her disappointment.

Setting his shoes on the floor, he turned back and flipped on the overhead light. No. If he was going to find the proof of his innocence, she would just have to agree to come with him.

He marched through the house, flipping on lights as he went. Marc hoped she wasn't sleeping too soundly, but he couldn't let that stop him. She had to hear him out. He had to make her listen.

When he pushed open her door, he was surprised to find Dana fully dressed and on her feet.

"Changed your mind?" She was checking her gun and didn't look up at him.

"You knew?"

She chuckled deep in her throat. "It's what I would've done if I were you." Stashing the gun in a holster at her shoulder, she shrugged on a jacket. "Mind you, I never would've let you get out of the yard without me…but I'm very glad you decided to come back on your own."

Marc cleared his throat. "Are we going to Chastain's office together?"

"No. That would be illegal—and probably useless. If there's anything incriminating of Chastain's that we can use, it'll be encrypted on his computer and not laying around his office for anyone to find. I think in Chastain's case, we'll be better off letting the Bureau tail his movements and get a warrant to tap his phone and computer."

"Then, where are we going?"

Dana finally looked over at Marc and felt the jolt clear down to her toes. When dressed in a suit and tie like he'd been earlier today, the man was devastatingly handsome. But put him in jeans and a black pullover and the sight did wild and wicked things to her libido.

Damn, but she was sure glad he hadn't tried to leave her behind. It looked like Marc Danforth was turning out to be just as honest and trustworthy as everyone said he was. So how come he kept trying to hit on her in her most vulnerable moments? It couldn't be because he really thought she was beautiful, could it?

Exasperated with the direction of her thoughts, Dana pulled car keys out of her backpack and sidled past him into the hall. "We're going to check out that newspaper warehouse on Montgomery Street. I'm sure Steve's gotten permission for us to enter it by now. I called him about it after dinner."

Out of the corner of her eye, she saw Marc narrow his eyes. He was beginning to figure out that she'd been planning this all along.

"Well?" she urged as she started down the hall. "Come on, Danforth. You're about to get your first lesson in surveillance. You'll love it. It's a barrel of laughs."

Three hours and four huge mugs of D & D Coffeehouse's extrastrong coffee later, the silence of the dingy warehouse was beginning to weigh on her nerves. Marc had been sitting still, with a pair of binoculars trained on the coffee suppliers' alleyway entrance for the last hour.

Dana did a couple of isometric exercises with her

calves and forearms and then decided to break the silence. "This has to be that boring time you were mentioning the other night. As long as we keep a careful watch, there's no reason we can't talk. How about telling me what happened a year ago that made you swear off dating?"

Even in the dark, she could see him grimace. "It's not a big deal, Dana. I didn't find out I had an incurable disease or anything, if that's what you're thinking."

When she didn't counter his snide remark, he seemed to finally give up his reluctance to talk. "All right. You might as well hear about my most embarrassing moment. If I don't tell you, you'll hear it from one of my brothers or cousins anyway."

He didn't take the glasses away from his eyes, but he relaxed back onto the stack of newsprint behind him. "A little over a year ago I thought I was the Danforth that had everything going. I was engaged to marry my college sweetheart. We were redecorating the farm so the two of us could start our lives there. I had recently been named Chief Counsel for my family's business. And my best friend from boarding school had just moved to the area to help me put together the family's new charitable foundation."

He took a breath. "Everything was right with the world."

"A charitable foundation?"

Marc nodded in the dark, but she could see his features by the faint light streaking through the dirty windows. "The Danforth Foundation. I wanted our family to stand for something important. Dad was willing. He thought it would be good for his political career."

"So what happened? Did you set up the foundation?"

"No." He took a deep breath and she knew he was steeling himself to say something that might hurt. "I…I was pretty full of myself at the time. Thought I was on the brink of a great life with the perfect woman. Thought I was better than my brothers and cousins who wouldn't or couldn't settle down and find someone who loved them."

"Pride has been the downfall of many men and women over the centuries," she whispered.

Shaking his head sadly, he grimaced. "Yes, well. I had it—in spades. Then last fall, I got lucky and managed to come home a day earlier than I'd planned from a fund-raising trip I'd taken with Dad. The condo was dark. I figured Alicia was already asleep so I took off my shoes and tiptoed to the bedroom."

Marc sighed, and hesitated to continue for long enough to make her afraid of what was to follow.

"I heard a noise coming from our bed that no man in love should ever hear," he finally said with a shudder. "When I turned on the light, there was my fiancée…in the throes of naked passion and…straddling my best friend."

Seven

Dana pressed her lips tightly together, trying to silence the cry that was forming in her throat. She knew Marc wouldn't want her to be shocked, or disgusted, or sorry for him. But she was—damn it. She was all those things and more.

How could anyone treat a nice guy like him that way? With all the bad guys she'd met in life, why was it that the one good guy ended up being the one that got shafted?

"So did you kill them?" she muttered. "No jury on earth would've convicted you if you had."

She heard him chuckle and was relieved to know she'd taken the right tack.

"No. But I have to confess that I considered it." He put the glasses down and took a slug of old coffee. "What I did was slink away to lick my wounds. I moved out to the farm, changing scenery to get away from the memories. And I dove into my work. I kept mostly to myself, except for a few charitable fundraisers and a couple of mandatory family functions."

He laughed out loud at his own misery. "So of course, I had to be the Danforth that Escalante chose for his frame-up. Nothing like a grand jury indictment to get a person back in the limelight…whether they want to be there or not."

Dana figured Escalante had picked on Marc because he was squeaky clean and made a good martyr. The papers ate up that kind of thing.

But Escalante hadn't counted on the FBI…and her.

Marc fell silent again, and she was content to quietly sit and think as the night wore on toward dawn. Dana made two definitive decisions. First, she was going to take down Escalante—personally. If she had to hound him for the rest of her life, the drug lord would never forget that he'd picked the wrong man to persecute.

And secondly, Dana vowed to be the one to bring Marc back into the world of caring relationships between a man and a woman. She had absolutely no experience with such things, of course. But she sure as hell could give it her best shot. For a man who simply oozed sexual energy, he'd been celibate long enough.

She refused to consider that maybe she wanted to explore their relationship for purely selfish reasons. No. It was much easier to tell herself she was doing this to save a good and kindhearted soul from his lonely and isolated life.

If Marc wanted her the way he said he did, then she

would be the first woman to let him know he was still a desirable man. A desirable man who didn't need a woman that came with an ugly background and no class. A woman like her.

Anyway, she knew the two of them would never be able to forge a lasting relationship. She was sure that Marc saw that as well as she did.

So she just must be the right one to bring him back his sexuality. Because of their wide differences, he wouldn't feel like he was obligated to her in any way. That should make things easier on him. He'd be free to make love to her and then go back to his life when she moved on with hers.

Yes. That was a sensible solution. It was a nice thing to do for a decent but terribly injured man.

Dana wasn't entirely positive she could become enough of a vamp to make him forget his past. But at the very least she had to try to help him heal. Knowing next to nothing about sexual things didn't matter when it came to Marc.

If she had anything to say about it, their pretend love affair was about to become very real.

"It's almost dawn," she told him softly. "We'd better get out of here before the neighborhood begins to wake up and we're spotted." She gathered the coffee mugs and folded the blanket that she'd spread out for them to sit upon.

"No one showed up last night," he grumbled.

"No. I'm afraid most surveillance is like that. Hours and days of boredom punctuated by a few minutes of sheer terror."

"Can we try again tonight?"

She cocked her head to study him in the gray light. "It might be better if we got another team from the FBI's new task force to take over the watch every other night."

He closed his eyes and made an effort to keep his voice low. "I have to *do* something, Dana. I can't…I can't just sit around waiting for someone else to save me."

"We'll keep you involved. I promise." She led the way to the back of the building. "Are you hungry? Sleepy? Need a shower?"

Marc stepped through the alley entrance and secured the door behind him. What *was* he besides being frustrated, he wondered?

Dana moved to the driver's side of her FBI-issued car and unlocked the doors.

"I'm just great thanks, Miss Mother Hen," he lied.

How had his life gotten so messed up? Feeling as helpless as he had when his mother died, he tried to think of what had worked back then that helped make him feel stronger? He'd only been a baby really, but he remembered that something had calmed him. What had it been?

He thought about his older brothers, misbehaving to act out their grief and frustration at not understanding their mother's death. But how had *he* managed?

It suddenly hit him. "Dana, have you ever seen the sun come up over the Atlantic?"

"What?"

Smiling, he buckled himself into the passenger seat beside her. "I suppose you have. But you've never seen it the way it is from Crofthaven. That's what I want to do. Do you mind?"

"What?"

"I want to go watch the sun come up from the private cove at Crofthaven. Okay?"

"Well, I guess so. We won't wake up or disturb anyone, will we?"

"There isn't anyone staying at the house now except the servants. Dad's on his campaign trip. In fact, it's the best place I know of to hide out. To think."

"Okay then," she grinned. "But I'd rather that you try to relax enough to get some sleep. You haven't had a lot of rest lately."

Sleep was the last thing on his mind by the time they passed through the gardener's gate and turned away from the main house toward the ocean. He was thrilled and excited to be going back to his childhood hidey-hole.

The midnight blue skies were just beginning to give way to streaks of rose and gold. A few storm clouds were out on the horizon. But that usually made for a great sunrise.

He directed Dana to park under a stand of salt pines, and led her down the rocky path between rows of sea grape and sand dunes. Marc hadn't been down to the beach in years. Hadn't managed to think of it much lately at all.

The smell of bracing salt air brought back pleasant memories of laying in the hot sand and playing in the light surf with his brothers and cousins. There weren't any bad ghosts here. No bad vibes to be heard over the screams of the gulls. Nothing here but the echoes of good times, roaring in his mind like the phantom sounds of waves when you put a conch shell to your ear.

"Oh it's lovely," Dana said when she stood at the water's edge. "Is it low tide?"

He shrugged. "Don't know. But we'll sit back a little ways, just in case."

Dana snapped her fingers. "The blanket. We need the blanket to sit in the sand. I'll go get it from the trunk." She turned and scurried back up the dunes toward the pines and her car.

Marc stood there watching her go, enthralled with the carefree way she moved. Her long hair swung wildly down her back, drawing attention to the curve of her hips.

He didn't feel much like himself all of a sudden. Maybe it was because he'd finally gotten that nasty story of last year's betrayal off his chest. He hadn't told the whole story to anyone before Dana, and saying it out loud made it seem more silly than despicable.

What he hadn't told Dana was that the more he thought about Alicia making it with Ben, the more he'd come to the conclusion that he hadn't really loved her in the first place. And wasn't it true that no relationship problem was all one-sided? He'd been so wrapped up in his new projects that he'd probably been ignoring Alicia's needs.

By now, he'd come around to deciding that he was grateful to Alicia for giving him a good excuse to end the engagement. But he wasn't exactly ready to forgive and forget where his old buddy was concerned. Ben's betrayal was the one spot that would remain sore for a long while.

Dana waved to him from the top of a dune and started down the path, bringing him back to the present. The sun was just beginning to climb over the bank of clouds on the eastern horizon, and the peachy-colored rays lit up the beach with a rosy glow. As he watched, the light shone on her face and turned her skin to amber.

God, she was beautiful. As she bounced down the path, she looked like a Gypsy with those big brown eyes, amber skin and those ebony curls making a halo around her head. She'd been so easy to talk to. He wasn't sorry that he'd told her the whole story.

As he helped her spread the blanket over the sand, Marc had a great sense of well-being. He remembered his grandmother saying that everything happened for a reason. Maybe he was the Danforth who was *meant* to be involved with the cartel so that the fates could bring him Dana. And maybe she was *meant* to be the FBI agent assigned to him so that she could bring him peace of mind.

It all sounded quite rational in his hypersensitive and exhausted brain.

Dana settled on the blanket, sitting cross-legged and focusing her gaze to the east and the rising sun. He kicked off his shoes and socks and sat on the blanket too. For fifteen minutes they sat quietly watching the sun cast a pinkish hue across the waves.

"Why don't you take off your shoes and get comfortable?" he asked her. The sun was warming the sand and he dug his toes in it like he had as a kid.

"Are you relaxing?" Dana took off her shoes and socks and laughed as she wiggled her toes.

"I'm getting there."

"Good." She shrugged out of her jacket and removed her gun from its holster. "I think it would be great if you could manage a short nap. You need rest in order to concentrate. I had a boss once that insisted all agents in his section stop work and get at least seven hours of sleep a day. He said the worst thing you could do for your health was to not get enough sleep."

"But *you* don't sleep that long."

"No," she agreed. "I've never needed that much sleep all at one time…high metabolism…I guess. But I do try to catch a couple of naps during the day. It clears my head. Why don't you try it?"

She checked the safety on her gun and placed it and the holster under the far corner of the blanket. "We won't be disturbed here, will we?" she asked, rolling up her jeans.

"No. This place is a private cove and totally out of the way. No one ever comes down here."

Marc was fascinated by her. Every action was liquid and smooth. He took off his jacket and decided it had grown warm enough to take off his pullover shirt, as well. Rolling them up, he bunched and stuffed the roll under his head as he lay on his back on the blanket.

He looked up at the puffy white-and-gray clouds in the sky and heard Dana sigh. He was afraid to glance over at her. Afraid that his desire would show too clearly if he looked at her now. And he'd promised himself that he wouldn't rush her. After all, she'd said she was here to work and not for play.

Resolutely, he closed his eyes and took a deep breath of salty air. It would probably rain later, he thought. This time of year the clouds came up off the ocean and soft fall showers cooled off the warm, sticky days.

For a few minutes he tried to clear his mind and

rest. But knowing Dana sat that close to him was a fact impossible to ignore—and it was beginning to make him sweat.

Finally, he turned on his side and propped himself up on one arm so he could look at her. She lay on her side facing him, eyes closed and her head resting on one arm. What a gorgeous picture she made.

Her coloring was the thing that riveted him. The golden skin and black hair. It was so unlike Alicia's blond blue-eyed elegance that he felt as though he was facing a children's action figure.

Dana was strong and focused, just like one of those children's heroines. The power of her personality drew him, even while she napped.

Silky black curls drooped over her cheek and curled seductively around her slender neck. The V neck of her T-shirt revealed the curve of one silky breast. He had to take a deep, big breath to continue lying still beside her.

Though it had been over a year since he'd felt the weight of a woman's breast in his hand, a man just couldn't forget such a thing. His body responded to the sight of hers with predictable results. He had to grit his teeth against the growing hardness of his muscles.

He forced his eyes to move on with their perusal, glancing down to the dip of her waist, the round hips that led to the impossibly long legs. A vision of those legs wrapped tightly around him brought his attention sharply back to her upper body. Lord, but he was longing to find satisfaction in that sweet body.

When his gaze ricocheted back to her nubby-tipped breasts, he noticed that he could see the hardened peaks distinctly through the material of her shirt. He shot a

glance to her face, chagrined to discover she was staring at him with heavy-lidded awareness. She never
moved, but held him with her steady gaze nonetheless.

An intense wave of yearning flooded his senses,
shooting heated blood to his thighs, hands and chest.
"I...I'm...I was just..."

She pressed her fingers to his lips. "Don't explain. I
like it when you look at me."

He could feel his heart hammering to a thick and
aroused beat. "I thought you said you didn't want..."
He cleared his throat and tried again. "But..."

"I know what I said." Her dark, sultry eyes held his,
while she tentatively lowered her hand to touch his
chest. "But you've changed my mind for me. I've been
wanting to touch you since the first moment I laid eyes
on you." She drew circles in his chest hair with her fingers, lingering over his nipples and then trailing down
to his waist.

Every nerve in his body was alive with feeling. He
moved his hand to her cheek, drew aside a soft curl and
tucked it behind her ear. But then that wayward hand
refused to turn away from the softness of her skin, the
line of her jaw.

He didn't know what had prompted her sudden
change of heart about them, but he wasn't going to
waste the opportunity.

He let his fingers linger on the velvet of her skin for
a moment more, then let them skip lightly down her
neck and farther, to the pulse beat at the base. She closed
her eyes, afraid to let her vulnerability shine through.

Her full, rosy lips were parted ever so slightly. The
restless way she arched her back made him positive that

she was feeling the same things he was. She couldn't hide from him. Not her vulnerability—nor her sensuality.

Swaying toward her, he felt dizzy and lost. He leaned over and gently brushed his mouth across hers. Just the lightest touch of lips was all he'd meant to do. But the velvety smooth pleasure of her mouth and the small, soft noise she made left his brain stuttering and stunned.

He took her chin with one hand and let himself sink deeply into the seduction of her mouth. She tasted of the ocean and the sky, of all the earthy and sensual things he'd ever loved.

He kissed her…and kissed her. The moist heat bubbled up between them just as the sweat beaded across the small of his back. Pulling them both to sitting positions, she threw her arms around his neck and pressed herself tightly against his chest.

"Let me touch you," he said against her lips. Rubbing his hands up and down her spine, he felt her shirt sliding over her skin.

She pushed back slightly and settled herself on her bottom. "You're sure this place is private?" she asked with a groggy and heavily impassioned rasp in her voice.

"Positive." He didn't waste a split second with dragging her shirt over her head. Taking in the full view of her, he groaned. "You are so beautiful."

A sheer white bra covered her full breasts. But not so much that it hid the darkened nipples, puckered and hard beneath his hungry gaze. Paralyzed with need, he sat frozen and stared at the tantalizing sight.

"Marc, please," she moaned. But before he could

move to please himself, Dana took his hands and drew them to her breasts. "Touch me," she begged.

He traced the dusky outline of her nipples with his thumbs, but kept his eyes trained on hers. Using the pads of his fingers, he traced around the edges of the bra and watched her pupils dilate. He wanted to go slow. Wanted to savor the flush of desire he saw on her face.

Honestly he did. But she was affecting him on a level no woman had ever reached before, and he wanted to know why. Why was this so different? Why couldn't he think past the erotic longings?

"You want more?" he gasped.

She nodded, but kept her gaze steady.

He reached around her back and unsnapped the bra. Then edged his fingers beneath the straps and tormented them both by gliding those straps down her shoulders in a slow, playful slide. She jerked her arms free and he let the bra float away.

Once again he had to take a breath at the sheer beauty of her body. He kept his arms at his side and looked his fill. She eventually moved to cover herself, but he grabbed her wrists and held her arms at her side.

"Part of the fun is looking, Dana. Don't hide from me. I love your body." He cupped her breasts with his palms and bent his head to pull one nipple between his lips, lapping her sensitive skin with his tongue. "Looking. Touching. Tasting. It's all naturally designed to make you feel good," he whispered against her skin.

He blew a hot breath across the tip of her breast, then nipped it with his teeth. She arched her back again and writhed as he tugged at her breast more insistently.

Looking up into her face, he saw her nostrils flare,

her lips part and her eyes flame with desire. She gripped his shoulders and dug her nails into his skin. The sensation threw him into an excruciatingly sexual arousal and blinded him with a blue haze of need.

Gasping for air, he pushed her backward, shifted his hands to her wrists and pulled them over her head. A kind of madness filled him. A madness born from her strong nature and from his year of celibacy.

He shoved a thigh between her legs and opened his mouth on her throat. Sucking her tender skin, he licked his way down the curve of her breast and flicked his tongue lightly over the sensitive skin.

She arched against him, bucking her hips and straining against his hold on her wrists. Oh, but the taste of her was more than he bargained for. He feasted on the sweet, salty and decadent pleasures.

Running the flat of his tongue around her belly button, he sucked, lathed and nipped with abandon. When Marc ran into the waistband of her jeans, he opened the zipper with a quick rip before either one of them could think about it, dragging the denim down over her hips and pitching it over his shoulder.

He was lost in her softness. In the little cotton and lace panties she wore and the quiver she made when he covered her mound with his mouth. Kissing his way down one thigh and back up the other, he delighted in her strangled cries and the dampness at the juncture of her legs.

Clutching at his hair, she tugged him back up her body and kissed him with a violent need. Marc loved that she seemed as frantic as he was. Dana, the tough FBI agent, desperate and wild with passion for him.

He was helpless to do anything else but meet her demand for demand. When she reached for his zipper with trembling hands, he helped her by shifting to rid himself of the clothing. Then he straddled her hips, bending over to take her breast into his mouth one more time.

Her eyes grew suddenly wide and she reached for his rigid sex. She touched the tip, running her finger down the smooth shaft with pleasure. A bead of moisture erupted under her touch and he had to move away from her before he lost it altogether.

Reaching out to him with both arms wide, she writhed and moaned. "Please, Marc. Please."

He took the invitation, pulling her panties off with abandon. She spread her legs and he touched her intimately, judging her readiness. Hot. Wet. And inviting.

Her hands moved over his chest, finding his nipples and running over his muscles. Bracing himself with one arm, he urgently caught her buttocks with the other hand and lifted her hips toward him. At last. He entered her on an agonizingly slow slide, while a shudder tore through him at the tight, perfect pleasure of it.

Dana tensed against him. And it suddenly hit him that she was too tight, too tense.

He stopped, lifting his head to question her. "You're not a virgin. That can't be." He moaned with the shock of it and tried to gather his badly scattered wits.

"Please, Marc. I need you," she demanded with passion.

That simple but frantic plea might not have been enough to send him over the edge of reason. But then she wound her legs tightly around his waist, gripped him internally and arched once more, sending him spiraling deeper into her glorious warmth.

He found himself in a maze of heat and pulsing passion. With Dana swirling all around him—whimpering, begging, squirming under him.

"I...I can't..." Her sobs were those of a woman who was completely out of her element and didn't quite know...

He reached between them, flicked a finger over her center and dove into welcoming depths. Her cry was savage and feral as she shuddered around him. She dug her nails into his arms and bit his neck as her body continued to quake and jolt.

Marc loved the frantic joy in her voice, the ferocious animal-like movements she made. He pulled her up tight, thrusting violently—until he, too, let go. Until the world and all its problems were nothing more than dim memories. Until he and Dana were the only souls left on the face of the earth.

Throwing his head back, he howled with the welcome of his release—the passionate proof of his desire.

Eight

What have I done?

Dana couldn't catch her breath while her heart still hammered in her chest. It'd just hit her that making love with Marc was the most powerful…the most startlingly beautiful experience of her entire lifetime.

He pressed a kiss against her neck. A gentle kiss, it was filled with a tenderness that was threatening to break her heart.

In her head the whole thing had been way over the top. It wasn't supposed to be this way. Probably thousands of women lost their virginity every day. They couldn't all feel this same stupendous surge of… of…power. That was the only word Dana could think of that explained what she'd felt—was still feeling.

Marc had been crazy with his need for her. When she'd hesitated or when she begged for more, he complied with her every wish. She'd been the boss, the one in control. And he'd been the one to show her what her body was capable of feeling.

As if he sensed her disquiet, Marc lifted his upper body, leaning on his elbows above her. "Dana," he groaned. "Are you okay?"

She nodded, but had the feeling she wasn't going to like having any conversation with him right now. His tone of voice sounded guilty and full of regret. Dana wasn't in the mood.

"You were a virgin." He blurted it out as if it were an accusation—not like the statement of fact it was.

"True," she admitted. "But just leave it be. We don't have to talk. It doesn't matter."

"It matters to me." He idly stroked his hand along her shoulder and down her arm. "You're so...sexy...sensual."

The blazing morning sun made the red highlights in his brown hair gleam, sparkling like the glassy reflections off the top of the ocean's waves. He was so good-looking she nearly cried just staring up at him.

"Thank you. So are you," she managed on a half-choke.

His expression turned grave. "Oh hell, Dana. I thought since you weren't a schoolgirl—and you're an FBI agent, after all." He looked so exasperated and so adorable. "I was too rough...and I forgot to use any protection...and I didn't use my head at all."

He bent and murmured against her lips. "Forgive me."

"There's nothing to forgive." She tried to choose her words carefully. "Where I grew up, sex was a dirty word. If a girl was *easy,* she was just as likely to get gang raped as she was to snare a boyfriend. So, very early on I made a vow not to let any boy talk me out of my virginity…to become tough enough to fight my way out of potential hot spots. I learned to fight…not make love."

Dana twisted so she could look up into his eyes. "By the time I entered Quantico for training, the idea of being the world's oldest virgin was too humiliating to contemplate. I didn't dare date anyone who might tell the others. I just pretended that I had a boyfriend who lived out of town, and stayed to myself on off hours."

She swallowed and continued. "But this morning I wanted to be with you. When I saw you looking at me with that…desperation…and desire in your eyes, I wanted you to be the one. I gave myself permission to take what was offered—for the first time in my life." Touching the tip of his beautiful Roman nose, she let her finger wander down to trace the line of his lips. "And you were worth waiting for."

"Dana…" He sucked her finger into his mouth and pressed his body hard against hers, his chest brushing her breasts and their hips jamming together. "I thought I'd never make love to another woman. Just the idea of it seemed totally impossible after last year. But then suddenly—I *was* desperate for you. I'm still desperate for you."

Marc kissed her with a fierceness that stirred her soul, drinking from her lips as if she were his first sip of water after an impossibly long thirst. "I want more. Again and again," he groaned against her lips.

He moved his powerful upper body closer to hers.

Dana jolted as surprising new sensations began spreading from the point where his hard arousal pressed inside her body. She'd thought he would take a long while to recuperate. But all of sudden, he was moving, pushing, sending rippling currents of need and pleasure to every inch of her.

Slow and searing.

Marc stoked the fire between them once again as his lips moved across one breast at the same time he teased the other nipple between two fingers. Dana felt the fire ignite under her skin. Felt her mind growing soft along with her body.

The eruption of her senses came fast this time as he shuddered into her, gripping her tightly enough that the world spun and shook with wild explosions rocking between them. After all that, she thought that both their hearts must've stopped altogether. But he kept her secured in his arms and firmly rolled them over on the blanket together.

They lay sated and drugged with pleasure as the sun beat down on their naked bodies and the gentle ocean breeze caressed their hair. With her still cradled snugly against him, he closed his eyes and Dana listened as his breathing evened out and slowed.

She lay still and watched him sleep, then began to take inventory of what she was feeling. Nothing hurt. Nothing that is except a general achy feeling in the vicinity of her heart.

Dana gazed at the long smooth lines of his legs and hip, as he sprawled on the blanket next to her. The man was genuinely beautiful. She took in every inch until the torture of wanting him became a poignant, depressing pain running through her entire body.

Oh man, she'd really gotten herself in a world of trouble this time. Wanting anyone this much was bound to turn out wrong.

The sun dipped behind a cloud and Dana felt a cold chill run across her skin. They could never have a lasting relationship. She wasn't positive that either of them would even know how.

Their situation had just become impossible. Unless...she could find a way to go back. Go back to being a tough, law enforcement professional, using her knowledge and connections to help a man who needed her. Go back to nothing more than friendship.

Determined to somehow put aside what the last few hours had really meant to her, she eased out from under his arm and sat up. The sun eased through a hole in the clouds and she realized it must be nearing mid-morning. Sighing, she reached over and grabbed a handful of warm sand, letting it slip between her fingers like the minutes of the time they had left.

Her first experience of desire was becoming just a memory. It had to be put behind her and forgotten. That was the only way. The best way.

A gentle tickle, like the flutter of butterfly wings, moved across his skin and pulled him from sleep. When Marc opened his eyes, he remembered where he was. And he remembered...Dana.

She sat across from him on the blanket, fully dressed and slowly pouring sand over his body. "Good afternoon," she said quietly. "I wanted you to get enough rest. But as the day got later and the sky darker, I began to worry that it might rain on us."

He reached out, wanting to pull her to him for one

more kiss. He was still not completely shed of his drugged sense of need. Though his brain was still fogged over with sleep, he wanted to experience yet another taste of her.

But she scooted back—away from his touch.

A tiny sliver of dread replaced the drifting sense of lust he'd felt upon awakening. In the overcast light, he saw a purplish bruise along the base of her neck and noticed her lips were swollen from his kisses. He touched his own lips and wondered if he had that same well-loved look.

When he looked down and saw the faint scratches on his shoulders, their morning in each other's arms came flooding back to him in full, vivid detail. They'd been wild together. Savage and visceral.

After being numb for so long, well over a year now, it surprised the hell out of him just how much he'd felt with her. Marc had returned all the passion and all the tender caring he'd witnessed in her eyes when she looked at him.

He'd been beguiled by her need. Fascinated that the tough FBI agent had waited—and wanted him. And he'd been stunned to discover a new dimension to making love.

Each of them had wanted only to please the other. It was the way he'd always imagined it could be. She'd managed to soothe his spirit and go a long way toward healing his battered soul.

Marc wanted to explore this relationship much further. He'd thought he'd been in love before, several times. But all of sudden, with Dana he'd felt a closeness and a need that was beyond all of his experience.

She sat there a few feet away, obviously waiting for him to free himself from the last bounds of sleep. He searched her eyes, expecting to see the same sweet connection that he'd seen in them only a few hours before.

"You'd better get dressed," she said, coolly. "It's getting late and we have plans to make." Averting her eyes, she stood and brushed the sand from her hands.

"What's the matter?" he asked, his heart threatening to burst from his chest. "Talk to me, Dana, damn it."

Shaking her head, she took another step away. "Nothing's the matter. It's about to rain. And it's time we decided how to proceed with our investigation. I have some ideas I'd like to discuss with you."

"Wait a minute." He scrambled over the blanket, retrieved his slacks and quickly yanked them on. She'd turned her back and was staring up at the path, inspecting the way through the pine trees at the top of the dune. "Wait just a minute."

He reached out and took her shoulder, spinning her around to face him. "Dana," his voice cracked with emotion when he said her name. "Please talk to me. Are you sorry about what we did? Were you lying when you said you'd wanted me to be the one?"

When she looked into his eyes, he spotted that fleeting look of vulnerability again. Right before she shut him out with a frozen stare. "Not at all, Marc. I'm just glad the anticipation is finally over. You were very gentle and made the whole process quite pleasant."

Pleasant? He couldn't have felt more like he'd been hit over the head with a brick than if she'd actually slugged him with a real one. Funny how a sensible word like that could make such anger surge up and threaten to swallow him whole.

"What…" His voice left him and he had to fight to get it back. "What are you trying to tell me, Dana?"

"I'm not trying to tell you anything," she said, as she pulled her shoulder loose from his grip. "We had a great morning, but that shouldn't stop us from working together and finding the proof of your innocence."

Damn it. That almost sounded right. Everything she'd said made sense if he could get his ego out of the way. Besides, he believed that her real motivation to be here was solely to get her job done, not to make him feel loved. After all, they hadn't made each other any promises.

But then…why did it hurt so much when she brushed their time together off so cavalierly?

Stupid. Stupid. Stupid. He couldn't believe he'd let a woman get to him again—twice in one lifetime. What an idiot he must be.

From now on, he would steel his heart whenever he was near her—or any other woman that could have that kind of power over him. He was sure he could live through this—no matter how badly it hurt at the moment.

He'd take advantage of Dana's friendship and let her help him out of his problems with the cartel. But that was as far as he would go. He wouldn't take another chance with his heart. No way. Never again.

"Sounds good to me," he grunted as he picked up

the blanket and shook out the sand. "Let's go make plans. The sooner I can be free of this mess, the better I'll like it."

The next few days went by in a whirl of looking at mug shots, doing busy work at the office, and waiting for the cartel to make a move. The frustration building in Marc's chest was threatening to explode. Something had to give soon.

He'd made a point of giving Dana her space, and hadn't so much as touched her since their morning on the beach.

Mostly he was afraid to touch her. Afraid of the electric zing in the air every time she came near. No matter what his head told him about protecting his heart, his body still craved hers. And his chest still felt like exploding whenever he spotted the soft curve of her lips as she became lost in thought.

Sticking by her side throughout the days and sleeping down the hall from her throughout the nights was taking its toll. The more they were together, the more muddled and confused about her he became.

But he wasn't in the least confused about Escalante or that damn assistant federal prosecutor, Chastain. Escalante continued to remain silent, and had ever since Marc's phony engagement was announced. But lately Chastain was giving public interviews about the pending case against Marc, and the need to revoke his bond.

Marc figured it would be but a few days before he ended up back in a jail cell, if Chastain got his way. "No one has seen Chastain going in or out of the coffee suppliers's office lately, have they?" he asked Dana as they sat in Ian's office waiting for a meeting.

"No. And Steve tells me they're having trouble getting a judge to issue a warrant for searching through Chastain's computer files."

"What? Why?" It had been days now and Marc's only salvation was the thought that somewhere—someone was getting the info that would clear him.

She shook her head. "It's complicated. Ordinarily, the federal prosecutor would be the one to present our request to the court. It can't happen that way this time. Steve doesn't want Chastain to get wind of what we're doing. The last thing we need is to alarm Escalante by making a mistake with the government official he's been paying off."

The panic rose up fast and quick inside Marc. "We have to do something," he urged. "We've only got a few days left before Ian's deadline. I can't let my family or our company suffer just to get me off the hook. It'll be the ruin of all of us in the end. We have to act, right away."

"I couldn't agree more, little brother," Ian said as he walked into the office and went to his chair. "But I'm afraid that SAC Simon and I disagree about what our next move should be."

"What move?" Marc asked as he slid forward to the edge of his seat. "Whatever the plan is, Dana and I should be let in on it. We're right smack in the middle of the…"

Marc trailed off when he glanced at Dana and realized the look on her face said that she had already heard about the plan. He must be the only one still in the dark.

Turning his back on his older brother, Marc twisted around to face her squarely. "Okay, Dana. What's this plan? And why didn't you think enough of me to include me in the discussions?"

"I…" Dana had the good grace to look embarrassed. She refused to look him in the eye.

"Marc," Ian said sharply. "Dana's on our side. Her boss insisted on running the plan by me before he approached you about it. I'm the one that has been contacted by Escalante. But you're the one that can…" he broke off and shook his head.

"Tell me."

"Steve wants you to contact the cartel," Dana told him in a clear voice. "He wants you to pretend that you've had a disagreement with your family and are willing to do business with the cartel behind their backs. You're supposed to give them the story that because of your impending marriage—" She stopped and drew a breath. "You want to stay out of jail and would like to make a pile of money doing it. And…you need to set up a meeting to discuss your deal."

"Great," he blurted. "Sounds like a good plan."

"Marc," Ian said in a low, dangerous voice. "It isn't that simple. Simon wants you to insist on talking to the head man. He wants you to say that you'll make a deal, but only with Escalante himself."

Ian shook his head slowly. "Escalante never meets with anyone, brother. You're as likely to be killed or kidnapped as you are to get an appointment directly with him."

Dana couldn't stand another minute of watching Marc try to cover up the expressions on his face. For days now, she'd wanted to comfort him. She'd known how frustrated and stressed he was over not being able to find the information on the cartel that would save him and his family.

She reached out and took his hand. The familiar jolt of recognition shot through her. But with a quick blink of her eyes, she covered her own reactions—better than Marc had been covering his, she hoped.

"Give me another day or two, Marc," she begged him. "I'll keep searching until I find the information we need. Steve will have to think of something else, or give us a chance to do some more research."

He pulled his hand from hers and stood. "The FBI's main objective is to capture Escalante, right?"

She nodded, uneasy about where he was headed with this.

"And if I help you accomplish that end, the Danforth family will be totally off the hook? The FBI will provide protection in case of any retribution from the rest of the cartel?"

"Yes, but—"

"I'll do it. Call your boss and get the plan finalized. But make sure it happens sooner rather than later. I've had all I want of Escalante, the cartel…and the FBI."

He'd emphasized that last little bit for her benefit. She knew that he meant that he'd had enough of her hanging around. The last few days had been uncomfortable for both of them.

She'd thought that by making love with him she would help him get over the hurt feelings caused by his ex-fiancée. Instead, the pain in his eyes when he looked at her said that he'd been even more hurt by being with her.

Dana had no idea of what she'd done to hurt him this

much, or how to get the two of them back to being friends. Or how to make up for whatever pain she may have caused him.

Romance. Sex. Even pure friendship was beyond her experience.

If only Marc had been a bad guy. She would know what to do about him then.

As it was, she had no choice but to continue on with her job. Save Marc and capture the drug lord.

But damn, it was hard to do when she looked into his darkened eyes and saw that tender look mixed with anguish. Or when she caught him staring at her in quiet moments. Or when her heart broke as she heard him pacing the floors of his bedroom all alone in the middle of the night.

She had to find some way of giving him back his dignity and taking away the hurt she'd unknowingly caused.

Setting her jaw, she said the words that might end up being the hardest ones she'd ever tried to live with. "All right, Marc. I'll arrange things with Steve for tomorrow."

"But, Dana—" Ian interrupted.

She held up her hand to silence Ian's objections, while all the time agreeing with his sentiments. "We'll take every precaution to protect your brother. I'll be with him every step of the way. Nothing will happen to him. And if we're lucky, by the day after tomorrow, this whole nightmare will be over for the Danforths."

Just saying the words hurt her deep inside. Nothing would happen to Marc while she was on the job, there would be no fear of that. But she wasn't so sure about what would happen to her heart once this assignment was finished.

Maybe a lifelong lonely nightmare was just beginning.

Thank God Dana had to leave him alone at the office for a few hours. She'd gone off to meet with her boss and put the finishing touches on their plan.

Another few minutes of having to be near her and yet not being able to touch her would've killed him for sure. Marc was glad this whole deal was coming to a head. He couldn't bear the daily reminders of her lack of feeling for him.

Hell. He knew he should amend that. She did care— a little. At least, she felt about him the same way she would've cared about any victim of a crime.

But it wasn't enough. He wanted her to touch him the same way she used to—like she couldn't get enough. Or to soothe his brow when he was frustrated. Or to smile at him when he was at his worst.

He shook his head and frowned. Hadn't he learned anything?

Yes, damn it. He'd learned that he had no one to count on but himself and his family.

Idly he rummaged through the messages that had piled up on his desk. The family was all in a tizzy over his predicament and over his very public engagement announcement. Every single one of them had called to offer advice and solace—or help.

One message caught his eye. Lea, his newfound half sister, wanted him to call if he needed anything.

He'd felt particularly close to Lea when they'd first met. The two of them were near the same age and both had lost their mothers.

Lea and Michael Whittaker were married now. And Michael probably felt he owed Marc something for allowing the FBI to use his name and business as Dana's cover.

But Marc was sure that Michael had only done it with the best of intentions. Everyone in the family wanted to do anything they could to help…and Michael was no different.

However, it wasn't Michael that Marc needed right now. It was Lea and her computer skills. Lea knew every sneaky way in and around the Internet. She'd already proven her expertise several times in the recent past.

He picked up the phone and dialed her number. "Lea, I need a favor—if you think it can be done."

"A favor?" she repeated. "You've always been very kind to me. I'm your sister, Marc, and I'll do whatever I can for you. What do you need?"

"Information from the Internet, and I'm pretty sure it's not legal. Does that make a difference, sister?"

Lea laughed into the phone. "Not much. Tell me what you want done and let me decide how much trouble it will be." She laughed again. "You'll defend me if I get caught, won't you?"

"If I don't get the information I need, I might not be in a position to defend anyone." He said the words with a chuckle. But in truth, if the FBI cleared his name without also proving that Chastain had participated in framing him, Marc's reputation would be ruined. And it was possible that he could still be barred from practicing law forever.

Nine

Marc made a point of not telling Dana about Lea and her promise to use the Internet to find incriminating evidence against David Chastain. He was certain Dana would not approve—and she might try to stop them.

Later that evening Dana picked him up from work. The FBI's plans had been made and phone calls to the cartel were scheduled for later that night.

In the meantime, the two of them went back to the farm. But first, they stopped and picked up a couple of pizzas and a six-pack of beer to go. He wondered if this might become his last meal. So, he got exactly what he wanted, ordering his pizza with ham and pineapple.

Dana, on the other hand, thought that was a terrible combo, ordering hers instead with "everything"—including extra sausage. "A pizza is simply not a pizza without extra sausage and anchovies," she grinned.

"That's what I always order when I'm undercover. It's a tradition before a big sting."

The pizzas turned out to be a bad idea. When a long and limp cheese string lingered in the air between her hand and her mouth, all Marc could imagine was licking it off of her fingers, her chin, her lips…

He'd never thought of pizza as particularly sensual before. But with Dana, it was an aphrodisiac of the gods.

She took her first swig of beer and foam appeared like a mustache on her upper lip. As she stuck her tongue out to clean it off, his libido went into overdrive.

That was just about all he could stand. "If we have a couple of hours to wait, I'd like to go see Laddie." He needed to get out of this confined space with its lusty smells of Italian spices and warm cheese—and breathe in the fresh crisp air away from temptation.

"That sounds like a great idea. Hold on and I'll get my coat."

Hell. He'd wanted a few minutes away from the sights and smells of the woman that had been driving him to distraction. Instead, he would be taking his temptation—and his heartache—along with him.

He needed this whole cartel operation to be finished so he could put his life back into the box he'd made for himself over the last year. Only this time, he swore he would never be tempted by another sexy lady who wanted to use him and then dump him flat.

Dana was glad they were taking a brisk walk from Marc's farm to the neighbors'. Being cooped up alone with Marc had begun to wear on her nerves.

Laddie jumped and barked, straining against the

neighbor's chain-link fence when he spotted them. But as they came near, the dog turned into a perfect gentleman. He rubbed against her leg and put his nose under her outstretched hand, whining in recognition.

It was the first time that Dana had ever felt close to an animal. What a good friend Laddie had turned into. She wanted to bury her face in his fur, tell him about her troubles and have a good cry.

Good cry? Was she nuts? Imagine a tough FBI undercover operative needing to talk to a dog. Allowing herself to make love with Marc had obviously stirred up her emotions. She already knew the mere idea had stirred up her previously nonexistent sex drive.

Straightening her spine, she took a deep breath and let Laddie acknowledge Marc. The two of them roughhoused and then Marc threw a stick and the game was on.

But within a few minutes her cell phone rang and Dana had to break up the game. It was time for Marc to place the call that would set up his meeting with Escalante.

Thirty minutes later the time and place was all set. The great drug lord had insisted on having everything his way—a meeting this very night and at the place of his choosing. But hopefully, Escalante still didn't know he was actually dealing with the FBI.

At four o'clock the next morning, Marc would be risking his life so that they could capture the infamous kingpin. And she would be there in the shadows to make sure Marc survived. Their time together was almost over.

Whispering into her walkie-talkie, Dana positioned herself behind a Dumpster where she could keep Marc in full sight when he drove up. The meeting was to take place at a remote office building in the outskirts of Savannah. Smart and devious, Escalante's choice would be difficult to defend.

But Steve had placed snipers on distant rooftops and stationed a few men in nearby trees. Her boss had also hidden microphones both inside and outside the offices in order to catch whatever was said.

Because of the layout, there could not be any agents hidden within the office space. But she knew the team would only be seconds away. And she was here to make sure nothing went wrong during those empty few moments.

She crouched down and took shallow quiet breaths, hoping no one could hear her heart beating. Her stomach rolled as the smell of garbage assailed her nostrils. Fine time to suddenly get overly sensitive to bad smells, she chided herself.

After a few minutes, a low, black sedan pulled up at the far end of the building and a man dressed in dark clothes got out. Alone. It was not Escalante, who never traveled without guards.

The man checked his weapon then made a sweep of the building's perimeter with his flashlight. He barely missed spotting her in his hasty survey. Finally, unlocking the door, he moved inside the building. Through her earpiece, Dana could make out his movements as he checked each room.

The earpiece hummed again as all of her team quietly checked off their positions. Everything was set to protect the man she loved.

The man she loved? Had she really just thought that?

She couldn't love Marc. It was impossible! The two of them were as mismatched as two people could be.

As a teenager, she'd vowed never to let herself get stupid over any man the same way her mother had. So what was she doing now? She was about to take part in an operation where many lives might be at stake. And all she could think about was being in love? If that wasn't stupid, she didn't know the meaning of the word.

Twenty minutes later, Marc's SUV pulled around the corner. He parked in front of the black sedan, stepped out and covertly looked around, as if he was trying to spot the snipers he knew were there to guard him. She wanted to remind him of his promise not to give away the plan, but it was too late for that now.

Instead, she stayed silent. Her heart shifted at the very sight of him while he rolled his shoulders, straightened up and headed for the door. He was so brave to walk unarmed into what could easily be an ambush.

She checked her Glock, flattened herself against the wall and inched closer in the shadows near the door. With just one man inside, she wasn't concerned about an attempt on Marc's life. What worried her was the possibility that Escalante's man would insist on changing locations and try to talk Marc into going with him. That would create an untenable and dangerous situation.

Marc had been cautioned against it. She just hoped he remembered all of his instructions. His life was too valuable to take any chances.

Just as Marc reached for the door handle, the man dressed in black opened the door from inside and stepped out onto the pavement. He pointed a gun in

Marc's direction and told him to keep his hands where they could be seen.

She was only several feet away and could hear everything they said.

"Get your hands higher and turn around, Danforth," the man growled in a strong accent.

He patted Marc down, looking for weapons or a wire. Thank heaven Steve decided against trying to plant a wire on Marc's person. It might have cost him his life.

"Where's Escalante?" Marc grunted as he turned back around to face the gun. "I don't deal with underlings."

The man raised his chin and grinned. "You'll get what you asked for, gringo."

Static burst through Dana's earpiece as she heard one of the lookouts reporting in. "A dark van is turning into the target lot from the north."

A second voice reported in. "A limo is approaching target's position from the south."

The hairs on the back of her neck stood straight up. It was beginning to look like this would be some kind of ambush. Damn it.

Both vehicles rounded the building's corners at the same time. She held her breath and prepared to spring into action.

The van pulled up directly in front of Marc, and effectively blocked the snipers' lines of sight. As the van's back doors popped open, the limo pulled right in front of Marc's SUV and put it into a tidy box.

Suddenly, the entire parking lot was filled with brown-skinned men carrying machine guns. And every gun was now pointed at Marc. Her stomach took another twist and she swallowed hard.

An unarmed man she recognized from a mug shot as Sonny Hernandez, Escalante's right-hand, stepped from the limo and spoke to Marc. "Glad you followed instructions, Señor Danforth. No guns. No cops. Maybe Señor Escalante will be able to deal with you after all."

"Where is Escalante, Sonny?" Marc demanded. "He's supposed to be here. My meeting is with *him*."

Sonny chuckled low in his throat. "My boss is a very busy man...and very careful. I'll take you to him now." He gestured to the open door of the dark limo. "Get in."

Marc shook his head and took a step back. "No deal, Sonny. I'm not going anywhere. The meeting is here with Escalante or nowhere."

God, he was brave. But he was also in big trouble.

Every eye was on Marc as he maintained his ground. So Dana inched out into the glare of the parking lot lights and moved to within three feet of where he stood with armed men at both his back and front.

"You have no choice in this, Danforth. You and all of your family have never had any choice." Sonny pulled a weapon from his coat pocket and pointed the barrel at Marc's forehead. "Now get in."

Out of the corner of his eye, Marc saw Dana moving into the light. He wished she would've stayed in the dark. Absolutely positive he could handle anything these goons dished out, Marc needed a few more minutes to get Sonny to admit he'd been framed.

"No way." Marc shook his head again. "Escalante may have framed me, but he can't force me into a deal unless he shows up in person. Those are my terms."

Sonny laughed, shrugged his shoulders and cocked his gun. "*Estúpido*. We don't need you. No terms. No deal."

Uh-oh.

Everything happened in a blur of motion and noise. A gun was fired and Marc ducked. From behind him he heard a loud thud and a groan, but he was crouching and moving too fast to stop and check it out. He headed for the last place he'd seen Dana.

He saw her slightly behind him then, standing and firing at one of the thugs holding a machine gun. Fantastic! And still too far away.

"Get down!" she yelled.

His feet wouldn't carry him as fast as he needed to move. He felt like he'd already been weighted down with cement shoes. Not a good image.

"Halt! FBI. Everyone lay down your weapons." The disembodied male voice echoed around the parking lot like a voice from God.

But Marc was the only one to actually come to a halt. Everybody else either twisted, turned or started running. Loud explosions from various directions deafened him and gunsmoke blinded him.

The smell of sulfur burned his nostrils as he heard a shot whiz by his cheek. From nearby, a low groan that sounded like it had come from a woman echoed in his ears.

Dana?

He couldn't see her, couldn't see anything but smoke and haze. Oh God, not Dana. Please.

He found the wall of the building and felt along it, going in the direction of where he'd seen her last. Visions of her swam in his mind, filling him with mixed emotions.

The strength in her mind and body had originally amused and interested him. The vulnerability in her eyes when they'd made love had inspired him and made him want to keep her close. Her cool brush-off of his tender feelings afterward had knifed through his soul and made him want to shut her out of his heart.

But none of it compared to his current state of absolute panic—this terrible desperation to make sure she was all right.

He tried to fight the knot of tension that was threatening to buckle him over, and choked out in an urgent whisper, "Dana? Where are you?"

Through the haze, he saw her moving toward him. She was holding on to her left arm with her right hand, the one still carrying her gun.

As she came nearer, he saw it. The small bloodstain on her upper arm that was blooming like a crimson tide.

"My God! You've been shot." He took two steps that brought him to within inches of her.

"It's nothing but a nick," she whispered in a hoarse voice. "Get behind me."

Marc was close enough to feel her heat and hear her labored breathing. Close enough to see that her pale skin was covered with a light sheen of sweat.

"No, Dana, look at me." He reached out, trying to gently turn her to face him. Meanwhile, the gun shots and yelling continued unabated in the background.

With his first touch, she spun around and her face turned as white as a sheet of paper. Then her eyes rolled back in her head. On a murmured groan, her knees wobbled as she began to slip away from him.

He grabbed her up in his arms, keeping her from landing on the ground. Bending to his knees on the rough pavement, he tried to shield her unconscious body between his own and the wall behind them.

No matter what, she had to survive this. He'd never be able to live knowing that she'd died trying to prove his innocence. Swallowing past a lump in his throat, it dawned on him that he wouldn't want to live in a world that didn't have her in it.

As he held her close, listening for heartbeats and praying to hear her still taking breaths, he thought about how much she'd come to mean to him in such a short time. Regardless of the fact that she didn't want him, she'd become a part of his soul. Maybe the best part.

Before that thought really registered in his jumbled brain, a sudden thump of pain rammed his shoulder. He closed his eyes and placed a kiss on Dana's smooth forehead, wishing fervently that they'd had just a little more time.

"I don't have the time to wait for tests," Dana complained loudly. "I'm fine, really."

"Just sit down over there with the other patients, Ms. Aldrich." The harried young man, a triage nurse at St. Joseph's Hospital emergency room, pointed to a row of uncomfortable looking plastic chairs and made it clear that he would soon be back to check on her.

Reluctantly, Dana sat down next to a young woman holding a sleeping baby. It seemed safer there than over next to the old man with the hacking cough or over by the little girl who was covered in angry-looking welts.

Dana's bullet wound had already been cleaned and dressed. She hadn't needed stitches. Like she'd thought, it was only a minor scrape. So why the doctor had insisted that she wait for blood tests and X rays was beyond her.

Marc was the one that had needed sutures and X rays. A round had stuck him in the shoulder. It had gone through a fleshy spot cleanly enough, but it left a good-sized hole where it came out. He was going to be in lots of pain for a day or two. But he was alive and nothing was broken.

She swallowed down the lump in her throat as she thought about him risking his life to save hers. It was the first time anyone had put himself in the line of fire for her benefit, his selfless actions made her feel warm inside.

Confused…and warm.

"You don't look so hot." The young woman next to her was watching her closely. "What ya in for, honey?"

Dana turned and blinked at the question. "Uh… I fainted and the doctor wants to do blood tests and take X rays. But I don't have time for such nonsense."

"How do you feel now?" The woman rocked her baby gently in her arms when the kid fussed in its sleep.

"I'm fine."

"You don't look fine. You look…green."

Dana's stomach rolled and clenched, making the sweat bead on her forehead. "To tell you the truth, my stomach's a little queasy. I guess it's from all the excitement of fainting."

The woman studied her for a moment. "You don't need any old doctor's tests to know what's wrong, hon. I felt just the same way during my first few months. I keeled right over in church one morning. It was pretty scary until I figured it all out, I can tell you."

"Figured what out?" Dana pressed her lips tightly together and wondered where the nearest restroom might be.

"Why, that you're pregnant, of course. Will this be your first?"

Dana's mouth must have fallen open in shock. Because when the next wave of nausea hit, she snapped it shut, slammed her palm over it and blasted out the emergency room door into the parking lot before she made a complete mess of the waiting room floor.

Pregnant? Couldn't be. Could it? How would she know?

After she had momentary control over her stomach once again, Dana decided she didn't want to take any tests just yet. She needed to think—needed to clear her mind before she had to confront test results.

She started walking, moving quickly away from the possibilities. Before she could think of results and futures, she had to get the immediate past straight in her head.

Yes, she and Marc had made love with no protection. She tried not to remember the tingling jolts of pleasure and the dizzying rush of hormones that making love with him had created. But she'd been trying not to think of them—of him—for days now with no luck.

So…yes, she guessed it was possible. After all, it would be just like her to become pregnant at the very worst moment in her life. Exactly at the moment when she'd finally come to the conclusion that being single and alone in the world was far preferable to letting her heart get kicked in the teeth by any man way out of her league.

But—a baby?

"A baby," she sighed. A baby would change everything—forever.

Dana ducked into a little café around the corner, went straight to the bathroom and washed her face. Then she ordered a cup of hot tea and a side order of saltine crackers.

And she thought about all it would mean to be a mother.

"I have something to tell you," she mumbled casually.

Marc was sitting on the side of his hospital bed the second morning after he'd been admitted, trying to figure out how to put on his shoes. The doctor had just released him and he couldn't wait to get out of the place. But now he had a serious problem with how to tie his damned shoes.

"I can finish getting dressed and listen at the same time." He bent at the knees and tried reaching for his shoes with one arm. When he forgot and moved his other arm, pain shot through him and he decided there had to be a better way.

"Uh…" he turned to Dana and really looked at her for the first time this morning. "On second thought, I can't get dressed at all without some assistance. Would you…?"

"Oh. Sure." She knelt down on the floor, sat back on her heels and put his foot in her lap.

All he could see from this vantage point was the top of her shiny ebony hair as she busied herself with the ties. But he'd gotten a good glimpse of her face a minute ago and was surprised to see such a huge change in her appearance.

Her eyes were rimmed with red as if she'd been crying. And faint purple smudges were destroying the delicate beauty of the skin beneath those deep brown eyes.

Her boss had told him that Dana's injury was minor. And Marc had asked her how she was feeling when she'd first walked through his door this morning. "Okay," she'd said.

But she didn't look okay to him. In fact, that same vulnerable look he'd glimpsed once before was back in her eyes again.

And he didn't like what that look did to him. He hated the tender, protective feelings that surfaced in him when she appeared to be so needy. It was ridiculous. She was an FBI agent, after all. Capable of handling everything and everyone that came her way.

And he clearly remembered that she was the one who had put a stop to their relationship.

Just like the rest of the women in his life had done.

Where had all that bitterness come from? He didn't like thinking of himself as bitter.

"I think I know what you want to tell me," he said with a surprisingly husky voice.

"You do?" She looked up at him from under those long dark lashes, but she didn't make a move to get up.

"Yeah. Steve was in last night and told me our sting had pretty much been a bust." Marc wished she would quit looking at him that way. "Escalante never intended to show up. And, Sonny, the one man that might've been able to lead us to him...and clear my name...is shot up so badly that he likely will never come out of his coma."

"Yes, that's true," she said softly and lowered her eyes. "I'm sorry, Marc. But we won't give up. We still have a few more days left to clear the charges against you."

He wanted to reach out to her. Wanted to kiss the fingertips on the hands that now were raised, imploring him to be patient. Wanted to take her in his arms and soothe away whatever had made her so upset.

But he couldn't. He just couldn't.

What a coward he was. Afraid of taking one more chance with his heart. Afraid that if she turned him away again, he'd be down for the count.

Dana heaved a heavy sigh and stood. "Well, there's something else I have to tell..." Her voice trailed off and she seemed so hesitant that he was back to wanting somehow to protect her. But from what?

"How bad is this?" he asked warily.

"I...I don't think it's bad," she stuttered. "Actually, I believe it's a good thing. I think. I hope."

Frustrated, he reached out and took her arm. "Dana, what is going on?"

She glanced down to where his hand touched her skin. He'd felt the electric connection exactly the same way she must've. But he wasn't going to back away just yet.

After she'd looked up into his eyes again, she seemed suddenly to get a shot of fortitude. Her shoulders straightened and her chin came up.

"I've been feeling ill for the past couple of days. And that fainting spell during the shoot-out was the first time that I'd ever blacked out." Her lips drew into a tight line. "I haven't been tested yet…but I think it all means that I'm pregnant."

Marc jerked his hand away from her arm. Stunned. Stung. Confusion reigned and made a blithering idiot out of a man who normally could talk his way out of anything.

"I…I can't…" He knew he was babbling. But, Lord, who wouldn't be? "Do you intend to keep it if you are?"

She drew herself up and shot him a withering look. "Of course I do. But I guess that pretty much tells us how you feel about it, doesn't it?" She backed up a step. "Don't worry, Marc. I'm not trying to trap you into anything. After your charges have been dropped, I'll just disappear from your life again. You can make excuses to the media about where I've gone and no one will ever see or hear from me again."

"Wait!" He shook his head to clear it and tried to focus on her again. "Just wait a damn minute here."

Ten

She'd expected some surprise from him. After all, Dana was as surprised as anyone. But she hadn't counted on Marc's first expression being filled with such pure disgust. A look that clearly said he'd be damned if he would be forced into a relationship with someone so…beneath him.

"Listen," she began unflinchingly. "I didn't trick you into having unprotected sex with me. As I recall, you were a willing participant."

The anger came unbidden, and she tried to stem her emotions to get through the conversation. It was the last time she intended to talk about this, and it would be senseless to make the man an enemy when they were still working to keep him out of jail.

"No…I mean, yes," he said grimly. "Whatever happened, we're in this together."

Together. It was such a foreign concept that she couldn't get her brain around it.

She raised her palm to shove away his words. "After we prove your innocence, we won't be in anything together. Don't worry."

"Don't worry?" he repeated. "Of course, I'll worry. I'm going to be a father. And the mother of my child says she'll just disappear—go back to being an undercover FBI agent and take my child heaven knows where?"

Now *he* was angry? Forget that. She didn't need his anger, or anything else from him, for that matter.

A muscle twitched at his temple. "What are we going to do about this?"

"There is no 'we'," she snapped. "I told you, I don't want anything from you. My child and I will be just fine."

"*My* child too, don't forget." He took a shaky step in her direction. "The very least you will do is agree to a settlement from me. We can talk about whether it should be in a lump sum or in ongoing payments. But when that's finalized we will also negotiate custody and visitations."

He narrowed his eyes and set his jaw. "Get used to the idea. You'll be having a Danforth and there's no way you're going to take him away from me and my family."

She'd made him furious, she could see that now. As usual she'd handled the whole thing wrong. Perhaps if she calmed down and tried to be reasonable…gave him a little more background. Then he would see that trying to share a child would be out of the question.

"My father kept making appearances in my life too, and it was the worst thing that could've happened for all of us." She lowered her voice and made an appeal to his good judgment. "He never gave me anything except trouble, and that includes his name. Don't you see? The woman who will be mother to your child is a bastard. The Danforths don't want that kind of black mark in their background."

He stopped, took a breath and stuffed his hands in his pockets. "What kind of trouble did he give you, Dana?"

Oh, for heaven's sake. She'd just told him the worst thing about her background and he was quibbling about words?

"Just trouble, okay? He was a big man when he'd had a few drinks, and he loved proving it with his fists. I had to call the cops so many times to save my mother's life that the neighborhood precinct became my second home. That's how I decided to go into law enforcement in the first place."

Frowning, Marc looked away and seemed to be considering his next remarks. "We both need to think this over for a while. Give it a chance to sink in. A child's life is not something we should decide about in anger or in haste."

All the steam had gone. He was right. There would be plenty of time after her mission was over to make him see the light and give them both the opportunity to continue their separate lives.

"Good idea. Let's let it rest until after we obtain the proof we need to get you off." She looked around the room. "Are you ready to go? I'll bring the car around."

He nodded and rang the nurse's bell. "I'll finish signing myself out and meet you downstairs."

Dana had never been so relieved to be out of anywhere as she was when she dashed down the hall to the elevator. Letting her shoulders sag, she allowed the tears to fall freely once the doors closed and she was alone.

Why had she let herself get her hopes up? Admitting finally that the real reason she'd told him was in hopes that he'd insist on marriage, she kicked herself for being so dumb. She was positive she would have no trouble caring for a baby alone. What she'd really hoped was that he would want to give his child his name. And eventually—give Dana his heart.

Marc had been hurt in love before, she knew. And it had just occurred to her that he was afraid. Afraid to let himself become vulnerable to a woman again.

That was just one more reason why they weren't cut out for each other. She would never again let herself be afraid. But the look on his face when he'd reminded her that the Danforth name was something to protect, would haunt her nightmares for the rest of her life.

Her dream of a having a loving family for the baby disappeared with that look. It had been a foolish dream, anyway. And hadn't she learned the hard way in her life not to expect too much from dreams?

So why was she so miserable now?

She was afraid.

He looked out his office window and began to put the pieces together. After thinking it through for the last twenty-four hours, Marc had finally come to the conclusion that Dana was afraid to trust anyone with her heart. She probably had good reason, too.

He wasn't so sure that he would've survived a childhood like Dana had. And here he'd been feeling sorry for himself all this time.

His own heart went out to the little girl she'd been, all alone and fighting for her life. He fisted his hands and jammed them in his pockets.

When she'd told him about the baby and made it clear she didn't want him to have anything to do with it, his back had gone up. He'd reacted with typical male dominance. His need had been to control the situation, control her. That made him no better than the father who had tried to control her with physical power.

Except…

The realization hit him like a cold dip in the Atlantic. He'd reacted the way he did because he was afraid of losing her and the baby.

Belatedly, he concluded that he wanted to have a baby with Dana. Because…he wanted a reason to spend the rest of his life with her. Because…he loved her.

Yes, that's right. He loved her. Loved her enough to let her wound him—if that's what she needed. Loved her enough to let her go—if he had to go to prison.

"Mr. Danforth?"

He came out of his Dana-induced fog and turned around to acknowledge his secretary.

"You have several messages, sir. Are you feeling all right?"

Marc stretched and winced at the echo of pain in his shoulder. "I've been better. But I think I'll probably live long enough to go to jail. Are any of the messages something I need to attend to immediately?"

"Most of them have been from family. Everyone sends their regards. Everyone except for two of them, that is."

"Oh? And which two would that be?" He had visions of a couple of his brothers or cousins making jokes with his secretary about being out of a job when he ended up in jail.

Without skipping a beat, his secretary relayed the messages. "Lea Whittaker called. She said she has some information for you, but she'll be out for the rest of the day. Call her in the morning."

Lea? He'd almost forgotten about asking for her help. But he would call Lea tomorrow. There didn't seem to be much hope of implicating Chastain at this late date. However, Marc was determined to bring that jerk down, even if he had to do it from a jail cell.

"Who else?" he asked his secretary.

"Your cousin, Jacob, left a message. He said to remind you that you'd promised to attend the Charity Ball for the Intercity Childhood Safety Commission. It's this evening and your father expects both you and Ms. Aldrich to be there representing the family."

He groaned under his breath. He'd forgotten all about the Ball. The ICSC was one of the charities that he'd planned to include in the Danforth Foundation. They were doing important work.

"Yes, all right," he said, dismissing his secretary.

Would Dana be willing to go with him to the Ball? Probably, he thought. She would think of it as her job. But she also might very well appreciate the things that the ICSC accomplished. The commission gave shelter to kids whose homes weren't safe. And they gave one-on-one caring to kids who'd never had anything like that in their lives.

He thought of how safe and loved he'd always felt at home. Growing up without a mother had been tough, but his family never let him feel unloved. Dana hadn't had the benefit of anyone's caring in the place where she grew up.

Here he was…about to go to jail. Dana was pregnant with his child, and he'd never be able to talk her into marrying a guy who'd be spending the next ten years in the clink. Never be able to talk her into letting him help support them. But he needed to do something.

Marc checked his watch. This morning, as she dropped him off, Dana had said she would be back to his office at lunchtime. He was safe enough here and he had another couple of hours.

He'd finally managed to think of something that could work. And there just might be enough time. He reached for the phone to call a lawyer friend.

Who knew?

She twisted around for a better view in the full length mirror. The gown Nicola had helped her buy managed to hug all her curves. Dana hadn't really known she *had* any curves. But there they were, reflecting back and making her look like some movie star.

She'd hesitated when Marc first asked her to attend the Charity Ball with him. Such things were so far out of her experience that she wasn't sure she could make-believe well enough to get through it. Going to fancy dress balls wasn't one of the covers that she'd needed for covert operations in the past.

Now, looking at herself wearing the long, gauzy silver gown and stiletto heels, and with her hair piled up on top of her head, she figured that she just might be able to pull it off.

Thank goodness her stomach had finally settled down. That whole baby thing had been such a fiasco. Pregnant. Really. How dumb could she be?

A quick trip to a doctor this morning made her realize that having tests done *before* you opened your big, fat mouth was far preferable to facing your stupidity head on. A slight case of food poisoning could only be confused with pregnancy by an total idiot. Or by her.

That was the very last time she would ever order sausage on a pizza. The mere thought of sausage would be enough to make her gag for the rest of her life.

But the one thing the experience *had* taught her was how wrong she and Marc were for each other. Regardless of the fact that she loved him with everything that was in her, his first thought had been to save his family's name. It hadn't occurred to him to marry her.

Well, he could just stew for a while longer about their nonexistent child. She intended to spend the few remaining hours or days of their time together having him cater to her desires. He'd been so attentive since she'd first told him, though they had not spoken about the baby again.

If the two of them were destined to never see each other after the next couple of days, she wanted their last, parting moments to be enjoyable. More than enjoyable, she wanted him to remember the taste and smell of her for a good long time.

She was perfectly aware that she would never forget him, and would never have another lover as gentle or as giving. So one more night of passion to remember could not be considered a bad thing. In fact, she intended it to be very, very good.

There was only one stickler in her plan. One huge, glaring problem that still refused to be resolved.

Dana had tried everything. Had pulled every string. Had called in every favor, trying to get Marc's racketeering charges dropped.

Though Steve had promised to give Marc a plea bargain deal if he participated in the sting, that federal prosecutor, David Chastain, refused to consider it. If only she could wrangle one incriminating piece of evidence to prove that Chastain was on the cartel's payroll. But the Bureau's hands were tied.

She'd already resolved to never stop trying to make a case against Chastain, though. Just like she would never stop until Escalante was behind bars.

And Marc had already decided he wouldn't allow his family to suffer because of him. He would rather go to jail than let Ian make any deals with a drug lord.

Everyone was being so damned noble. But Chastain had almost convinced a judge to revoke Marc's bail, saying that he was about to use his father's power and money to leave the country. The federal prosecutor's office had apparently also submitted new evidence that Marc had been recently seen in the company of a known drug lord.

Worse yet, her boss, Steve, was making noises about letting him go to jail for his own protection. The FBI thought he would be safer in solitary confinement than in her custody. Frustrated and miserable, Dana knew she couldn't hold the inevitable off for much longer. The way things looked now, Marc would be headed for jail by the end of the week.

She had to admit Marc would be better off in protective custody, where Escalante would have difficulty reaching him, than to be free and at the cartel's mercy. It was the hardest thing she'd ever done, imagining Marc's solitary confinement in prison. Every time the reality hit her, a shot of adrenaline made her hands jerk and her body tense.

"Hi. You almost ready?" Marc stuck his head through the door of the guest bath. "Whoo hoo! Just look at you."

Whistling, long and low and slow, he raised his eyebrows. "You look good enough to eat."

He should talk. Marc Danforth in a tuxedo was every woman's fantasy. Each minute she spent with him was like opening a brand new Christmas present. One that made her heart pound and her body tingle.

She twirled around and did her best curtsy, trying to cover the flush of need that reddened her neck.

Marc stood and stared for a distressingly long time, at last nodding his head and clearing his throat. "I'm not sure I want to take you out looking like that. I'd rather not have to share such eye candy with all those other guys who'll be at the Ball."

Dana smiled, but she couldn't make one of her normal snappy comebacks. She actually did feel pretty. Maybe for the first time in her life. But she wasn't comfortable with the image. She'd much rather go back to her sexy vamp image—the one he'd given her that day at the beach.

Maybe later.

"Uh. Give me a minute, will you?" Marc winked at her. "Meet me by the front door."

She nodded, grabbed her shawl and the teeny little piece of sparkly leather that was supposed to function as a purse. Way too small to hide a decent weapon, the darned thing was barely big enough for a lipstick and a cell phone.

Fortunately, her stub-nosed .38 was now securely strapped to her leg, slightly above the top of those thigh-high hose Nicola had insisted she wear. But the weapon would no doubt wreck the mood she hoped to create later. She would just have to remember to take it off before she made her move on Marc tonight.

"Dana," he said on a deep breath as he reached her side in the foyer. "Do me a favor?"

His voice was husky, and she realized he felt the same rage of hormones that was threatening to paralyze her. "Yes, of course," she managed.

He dragged his fisted hand from behind his back and opened it, palm up. "Wear these tonight." Two extremely large and extraordinarily beautiful diamond earrings lay twinkling and glittering in his hand.

Shaking her head, she backed up a step. "No…no I couldn't. Those are way too expensive."

"Who better to wear them than an armed agent? You *are* armed tonight, aren't you?" He was grinning like a silly fool, and she thought he was too adorable for words.

"Yes. Does that turn you on?"

Marc sobered as he stepped closer. "I'm always turned on by being around you." He took her hand and the zing of by-now-familiar recognition blazed through her fingers and up her arm. "Please wear the earrings. My mother left them to me to give to…the mother of my children."

Jeez. He would go and say something like that. "I need to tell you…"

"Tell me later," he interrupted. "We're running late. Meanwhile, wear the earrings. It'll make me happy knowing you have something on that belonged to my mother." He took her chin, lifting it so he could attach one of the earrings to her earlobe with the other hand.

Oh, God. She couldn't cry. Biting the inside of her cheek, she managed to remain still while he finished clipping on both diamond clusters.

Then he stood back to inspect his work. His eyes glinted with sensual appreciation, and she could feel the heat and hunger in him from four feet away.

"Oh man, is this ever going to be one long night." He took her elbow and hustled them both out the door. "Lets hope we can find a way to cut out early. I have big plans for you, little mother."

Dana kicked off her shoes and relaxed into the leather seat of Marc's SUV. It had been a long night. But also a wonderful, rather special night. So good, in fact, that she hadn't minded how badly her feet hurt.

"Did you enjoy yourself tonight?" Marc smiled but didn't take his eyes off the road.

"Mmm, hmm. Yes," she murmured with a lazy purr. "Though, some of the names are all jumbled in my head."

Marc had been so attentive the whole time, and he'd introduced her to every single person at the Ball as his fiancée. He'd made it an unforgettable night.

"You know," she began again. "I talked to a lot of people and most of them actually find time to work for the ICSC. They're not just contributors."

"Is that a dig at me?" he grinned. "Because if it is, you should know that I work at one of their shelters every chance I get."

"Oh, no," she said with a gasp. "I didn't mean you. One of the staff psychologists told me the Commission wouldn't exist without you. It's been your time and money that got the whole thing off the ground."

The way she was looking at him made him feel like a giant or perhaps like some kind of saint. And though that embarrassed him, his pulse raced at the sound of her raspy, sensual voice.

"I didn't do it all alone, believe me," he mumbled. "And they'd better be able to get along without me. I won't be giving them much help from a jail cell."

Dana didn't say anything else, but her eyes were sad as she turned away and fidgeted in her seat. Man, that was not the mood that he'd been going for. This night was supposed to be meant for celebrating, not remembering that his time was running out.

He would be thrilled just to see her looking at him again like she'd been doing most of the night—as if she could eat him alive. Instead, he'd managed to turn her mood somber and fill her expression with regret.

Marc parked the SUV in the back of the house. He needed to find a way to change her mood before he gave her his news. He didn't want her to think that he'd done this out of regret—instead of love.

As he punched in the security code, Dana's face brightened and she turned to him. "I could start working with the Commission in your place until we secure your release. When I come to visit, you can give me instructions about what you think needs to be done."

He stopped, lifting her chin so he could look in her eyes. "You plan on visiting me?"

She lowered her gaze and blinked. "Only until I can find the proof we need to get you off."

Marc dropped his hand, fighting the sudden urge to hit someone, preferably David Chastain. "What about your job, Dana? Won't you have another undercover mission by then?"

"I'll talk to Steve. Or I'll take a leave from the Bureau if I have to. There is no way Chastain and Escalante are going to get away with this."

Her face held such a look of pure determination that his heart stuttered in his chest. God, she was special.

Because she was barefoot and carrying her shoes in her hand, he took her arm and helped her inside. This was the perfect time to tell her. And then…well, he hoped to spend the rest of the night showing her how much he appreciated every thing she'd come to mean to him.

After he lit a fire and brought her a mug of hot chocolate, they sat down in front of the fireplace. "Are you comfortable?"

She smiled, nodding as she quietly sipped. "The hot chocolate is just perfect."

"Great. Because I have something good to tell you."

All of a sudden, her eyes clouded over and she had that somber look on her face again. "Before you say anything else, Marc. There's some news I tried to tell you earlier, and I think I'd better say it now."

Marc didn't want to hear any more bad news at the moment. The mood he'd been trying to create was hanging by the slenderest of threads already.

"No," he whispered as he put a finger to her lips. "Good news comes first. Later, you'll get your chance."

She widened her eyes and opened her mouth, but he shook his head firmly. "Later."

Dana dipped her chin in acknowledgment.

"Great." He reached behind him for the folder full of papers that he'd received by messenger right before they'd left for the Ball. "It was touch and go this afternoon as to whether my friend could get this all accomplished in one day. But we pulled in a few favors and got the County Registrar to sign off on it."

"Marc, what have you done?"

He tried keeping the wide grin from his face and held it down to a simple smile. "I've put the title to this farm in your name. You own the house and all the property now. I don't figure I'll have much use for it where I'm going, and I thought…"

The look on her face this time was pure horror. "You did what? How could you?" She jerked up and spilled chocolate all over her pretty silver dress.

Confused and surprised by her reaction, Marc stood and deliberately kept his voice under control. "I thought you liked it here. I didn't want you to have to worry about a place to live while I'm in jail. I wanted to give you a place to feel safe."

His mind was racing. This conversation wasn't at all like he'd hoped it would turn out. "Is it the animals? I've already sold them to my neighbor. You won't have to worry about taking care of them." He swallowed and took a breath. "Except for Laddie. I was hoping you would want to keep him. But if you won't have time, I'm sure the neighbor would be glad to…"

"It isn't the dog." She swung around and took off toward the kitchen with him trailing along behind. "Laddie's fine. Don't give him away."

Picking up the dish rag, she reached over with her other hand and ripped a few paper towels off the roller. "Why?" She spun around and headed back toward the sitting room. "Why would you do something like this?" she demanded over her shoulder.

He wanted to tell her it was because he couldn't do anything else for her. That he loved her. And despite being headed for jail, this was something he could do to show her how much. He wanted to say all those things, but he didn't think she would want to hear them from a man who couldn't ask her to wait for him.

"It's not like I expect you to hang on to the farm for me," he yelled, chasing after her. "You'll be free to stay here or rent it out. Or, hell, sell it if you want. It's yours. No strings."

When he reached her, she was frantically dabbing at the wet spots on the couch. "I don't want it."

He heard the catch in her voice and it nearly doubled him over. "Dana, the couch is fine." He gently turned her around to face him. "Tell me what's really going on here?"

"You're giving me the ranch because I'm going to have your baby, aren't you?"

Marc could tell from the hesitant expression on her face and the wary look in her eyes that the question was some kind of test. But he didn't know the right answer.

He had a terrible feeling that if he said the wrong thing, he might be losing something forever. "Uh…"

"Oh, forget it. I know that's what you had in mind." She pulled out of his grasp and stepped away, far enough that he felt the chill in the air between them. "Well, listen up. I'm not having your baby. I'm not pregnant. I'm the dumbest person you know and can't tell food poisoning from pregnancy. I'm not going to be a mother."

Lots of emotions zinged around all at the same time, both in his head and in his heart. "I'm sorry, Dana." His mind was racing ahead of his mouth. "I know you well enough to guess you'd already decided you were happy about the baby. I believe you wanted to be able to give a child the love and trust you never received."

Suddenly her eyes filled with tears. He couldn't stand to see her hurting so badly. "Dana, I didn't mean…" He took a hesitant step in her direction.

"Don't…Marc," she put her arm out as if to ward him off. "We both have things to think about. I'm going to bed. We'll be able to talk about it more clearly tomorrow."

And with that, she left him standing there, his heart still dangling in midair.

Eleven

"Yes! This is perfect." Dana flipped through dozens of printouts, more astonished every minute by the sheer volume of information.

Instead of having a relationship-ending talk this morning with Marc, they were both awakened at 5:30 a.m., by a phone call from his half-sister, Lea. Within fifteen minutes she was banging on the front door, carrying a stack of papers and folders at least ten inches thick, and demanding that they look at what she'd brought.

"Sorry, it's so early," Lea told them. "I have lots to do today and I thought you would want to see these files as soon as possible."

"Yeah, thanks." Marc stood next to her in his foyer, wearing nothing but a pair of sweatpants that were riding low on his hips.

Dana was also wearing a sweatshirt and pants that were warm and cozy. But the heavy clothes didn't account for the heat in her body when she'd first seen Marc a few minutes ago, looking both sleepy and dangerous with his morning beard and dream-tousled hair.

"Do you realize what Lea has here?" she asked him.

He tilted his head and tried to read over her shoulder.

"It's the key, Marc," Dana said breathlessly. "It's the key that's going to open the jail cell for you and lock away David Chastain for good."

Dana turned the pages around so he could see what she was talking about. Lea had listed transactions to and from offshore accounts that would prove beyond a shadow of a doubt that David Chastain had been receiving cartel money. She had also provided credit card receipts for trips Chastain had taken to Columbia.

But the absolute topper was a copy of a Statement Of Intent To File, from an exploratory committee created to fund the 'David Chastain for Congress' office. And the first signature on the board of directors was none other than Jaime 'Sonny' Hernandez. The same Sonny Hernandez who was lying, with wounds received at the hands of the FBI, in a prison hospital at this very moment.

"That's great, Lea," Marc said in a serious tone. He slowly turned to address Dana. "None of this is admissible evidence, you know. It was obtained illegally."

"Oh, I know." Dana was nearly giddy with relief. "But it's all we need to get a judge to issue search and seizure warrants so we can get the same information through FBI Intelligence units. And…"

Dana looked up at Marc's clouded expression and her heart flipped. "My boss can now go privately to the senior federal prosecutor for this district—David Chastain's superior. My guess is the charges against you will quietly be dropped by the end of today."

Marc took a deep breath and his shoulders relaxed. He turned his head, but not before she noticed a sheen of wetness appear in his eyes.

"Thank God." He dragged Lea into a bear hug. "Lea, how can I ever repay you?"

Lea grinned and pulled away. For a second, she studied Marc's ecstatic expression, then she turned to look at Dana. "Just be happy, brother," Lea advised. "Have a good life, you two. Don't take anything, or anyone, for granted."

Lea excused herself and left them both standing silently inside his front door. There was so much to be said—there was so little that they could say.

"I'll call Steve," Dana told him on a ragged breath.

"Okay. I'll go grab a shower."

Twenty minutes later, Steve showed up and took possession of Lea's files and printouts. "I wish I could've found a way to keep up my end of the deal before now, Dana. You know I do. But this evidence will wrap it up for Chastain. And I have high hopes that it'll spell the beginning of the end for the whole cartel."

He spoke quietly, giving her a few instructions in private. "Marc's still in jeopardy. Escalante may hope to get rid of him so he can deal directly with Ian. An execution attempt is not out of the question until we can wrap this up and put Chastain behind bars.

"We'll need at least a couple of days to gather subpoenas and make the arrest," Steve soberly told her.

Marc came down the hall from his bedroom and Steve shook his hand, congratulating him on the break he'd engineered for himself. As Steve prepared to leave, he stopped to address them both. "Stay here, don't answer the phone and don't let each other out of sight until I contact you on Dana's secured line. Escalante and the cartel are more dangerous than ever right now. I need you both alive so I can call on you as witnesses."

After Steve left, Dana locked the door, checked every possible means of entry or attack and reset the alarm. "We'll be all right here," she said with confidence. "It might be a little boring, but we're as safe as we could be anywhere."

Marc stared at her in silence, narrowing his eyes and raking his gaze over her body—from the tip of her uncombed hair down to the toes on her still-bare feet.

She'd forgotten how sexy he looked with his hair still wet from a shower. Barefoot, too, he'd pulled on a worn pair of jeans and a denim shirt that he hadn't finished buttoning.

Suddenly, the sight of his bare chest, his just-shaven face and his dark, searching eyes sent waves of sensation to her belly and then lower. "Uh… I think I'd better go get dressed before it gets any later," Dana stuttered.

He nodded sharply. "Yes…all right. I'll go see what I can hustle up for breakfast."

Dazed, Dana stood under the shower and let hot water sluice over her body. She tried to replay the events of the last few days in her head.

Something that Marc said had been important. But it was being elusive, just under her conscious level and right out of her reach. Remembering their talks about the baby and the farm, she went over and over his words.

He'd given her the farm. Wow. Just the mere thought of that still blew her away. She would have to make sure he reversed the title before she left for good.

But what kind of man would give his beloved farm away, anyway? It seemed much too generous, even for a man who thought he'd be going to jail and wanted to take care of his unborn child.

What had he said? Now she remembered. He'd said he wanted her to have a place to live, a place where she would feel safe. He hadn't mentioned the baby.

Oh, my. She dropped the soap on the floor as the truth dawned on her. Marc hadn't given the farm to his unborn child. He'd given it to her alone.

Years of law enforcement training made her want to try to come up with his possible motives. But the only motives she could find for a man who wanted a woman to feel safe were either a close friendship, a family relationship ... or love.

Was that it?

Dana stepped out of the shower and grabbed a towel with shaky hands. She knew he'd been hurt and wouldn't trust a woman easily. But obviously she must mean a great deal to him.

Was it love? Or a close friendship after all they'd been through together?

She quickly decided to try her own covert operation to find out which. After all, she'd already decided she loved Marc. And she knew she'd give her life for him. Wasn't he also worth taking a risk to her pride?

* * *

Marc forked the bacon onto a waiting paper towel. How in God's name would he ever be able to spend the next day or two locked up in this house with Dana and manage to keep his hands off her? Just thinking about her, wide-eyed with joy over Lea's good news, made sweat roll down his spine.

All night long, he'd tried to think of the best way to talk Dana out of her fears and learn to trust in him. This morning it seemed hopeless. She'd been emotionally bruised and hurt as a child by people who should've loved her. How could he ever expect her to leave it behind and accept his love?

He didn't think he could. And he refused to use sex, no matter how good it was, as a means to make her see how much he cared. It wouldn't be fair.

No. He simply would try to relax and let her enjoy her last few days. No pressure.

The only pressure would be his, trying to carry on conversations and remain neutral. When what he really wanted was to kiss her senseless, proving his love with tender touches and elegant moves.

Marc scrambled the eggs and poured them into the pan. He heard Dana come into the kitchen and clear her throat behind him. But he didn't dare turn around just yet. The erotic thoughts were clearly visible on his lower body.

"Do you need any help?" she asked.

"No, thanks," he muttered without turning around. "Get yourself a cup of coffee and have a seat. Breakfast will be ready in a minute." He stirred the eggs with one hand and slipped a couple of pieces of bread into the toaster.

"Marc?"

"Hmm?"

He heard her move across the kitchen floor toward the table. "When were you planning on reversing the title to the farm?"

"I wasn't planning on it," he said over his shoulder. "The farm belongs to you now, Dana. Just because I won't be going to prison doesn't mean I want to take back the farm. As soon as Steve says we're free to leave here, I'll go rent a condo in town. Then you can move your things in."

He pulled the first batch of toast out of the toaster and slid in another couple of slices, all without looking at her. "I don't imagine you'll have enough furnishings to fill this whole house, so I plan on leaving everything here. I'll buy some furniture wherever I go."

Scooping the cooked eggs onto two plates, he listened for her to make some snappy reply to what he'd said. But there was nothing except the ticking of the kitchen clock.

He turned to put the plates on the table. "Of course, if there's stuff of mine you hate, I'll get it out of your way. Just let me…"

Stunned by what he saw as he turned, Marc froze and stared at Dana. She stood beside a chair, dressed in a flimsy black robe he'd never seen before. Her hair, still wet from her shower, hung in soft ringlets against slender shoulders. And on her feet were those spiky high heels that he knew she hated. The ones that made her legs look long and sexy, and turned him into jelly with just one glance.

Her nipples were puckered and jutted against the

sheer material she wore. She looked like a woman who was dressed for love. Correction. Ready, willing, and *almost* undressed for love.

He knew his tongue was hanging out, and he heard himself panting through an opened mouth. As he dropped the plates on the table, a quick flush of need gravitated right to his groin. Only then did he finally gaze into her eyes.

And he couldn't believe what he saw. Tears pooled there. Big, sad, wet drops rolled down her cheeks.

"Dana?" In one huge stride he had her in his arms. "Don't..." He could barely speak.

"Please don't do that," he groaned against her hair. "Whatever's the matter, we can fix it together."

"You gave me the farm," she sobbed.

Confused and hurting, he fought his own tears. "Yes, and I'd give you the world if I could. But I didn't do it to hurt you. I'd die before I caused you any pain, don't you know that?"

"I'd die for you, too," she blurted. "I don't want to live here without you. I love you." She threw her arms around his neck and pressed herself against his chest.

He groaned with relief, and quickly tried to overcome feeling like he'd been hit in the heart with a two-by-four.

Choking back the surprise, he steadied his voice. "Well, isn't that a coincidence?"

Marc couldn't keep the grin off his face, but he pulled back and narrowed his eyes at her. "Because I love you, too, Special Agent Aldrich. Maybe you'd better arrest me before I steal you away, body and soul."

"You love me?" she asked in a shocked whisper.

The look in her eyes nearly threw him to his knees. She was putting all of her fears on the line for him, and at the same time needing him to wash them away with trust and love. It was the most precious gift anyone had ever offered him. Once again, she'd made him feel like a giant.

He kissed her softly. "I love you."

It was her turn to gasp in surprise. "But you were hurt so badly last year by your fiancée and your best friend. You said you'd never again let yourself…"

"Shush," he chuckled. "I said a lot of idiotic things. But that was before a gorgeous FBI agent came along and made me see that I was just desperate to be loved for real."

Her brows drew together. "I thought you must not want me when you thought there was a baby coming and you didn't ask me to marry you. I figured you were too afraid of getting hurt."

"I was afraid," he echoed. "I imagined I would go to jail before I could make you see that I wanted to take care of you and the baby. I was near panic with fear of what would happen to you when I went away."

Her eyes glittered, but then a frown creased her face. "Are you very sorry about the baby? That there is no baby?"

He leaned his forehead against hers. "Only if you decide you don't ever want to try for another one."

She leaned back and rewarded him with a grin. "Trying is the best part."

Marc laughed, nearly weeping with love for her. "Marry me, Dana. Today. Or as soon as Steve says we're free and we can gather the family together."

"Marriage? Really?" She pursed her lips and looked thoughtful.

"Just say yes, Dana. For pity sake." He dropped his chin and lasered a kiss across her lips. A kiss that carried all his hopes and love behind it.

Smiling when he let her up for air, she tilted her head and batted her eyelashes. "Uh. Do you mind if we have another test run of that 'baby trying' business before I make up my mind?"

He swept her up in his arms and headed for the bedroom. "Whatever you wish, madam."

"What about the breakfast?" she weakly protested.

"I have something better in mind to feed you." Both his body and his voice had grown heavy with desire the instant that he'd seen passion replace the fear in her eyes.

He sat down on the bed and settled her into his lap. "Now then, if this is a test…" He stopped talking and let his gaze rake over her body, long enough to appreciate what he saw and calculate his next moves. "Let's see what I can do toward earning a passing grade."

Her face lit up with anticipation and need as he stroked his hand along her thigh.

He slid his fingers under the elastic of her thigh-high stocking and slowly peeled it down, taking it and the shoe off in one smooth move. "You're wearing those heels I know you hate. Why?"

When she closed her eyes and ground her bottom against his erection, he could tell that her needs were every bit as strong as his own. "I…" Breathing heavily, she managed to open her eyes. "I wondered if what you felt for me was love or just friendship. I thought if I could seduce you…"

"What did you think?" he interrupted with a chuckle. "That if it wasn't love, we could have a friendly little roll in the hay?" Laughing, he noted that the sound he'd made seemed breathless and rather desperate.

Making short work of the other nylon, shoe and then her panties, he pushed aside the see-through robe and placed his lips on her silky shoulder. "Aw, honey," he mumbled against her skin. "I'd love to draw this out for you. Prove that what I'm feeling is really love. But…"

"Next time," she said huskily. She put her hands on his head and drew his lips down to one hard and puckered nipple, showing him that she too was desperate.

He shoved the robe and bra strap off her shoulders while his tongue swirled around her peak through the soft material of her bra. Sucking, lathing and nipping all at the same time, he lost himself in the short gasps she made in response. At last, moaning deep in her chest, her keening rumble urged him to move faster.

Marc sought the warmth between her thighs. When he found not only warmth but wetness there, he cupped his hand over her mound, moving his palm in a circular motion against the most tender spot. She arched her back and spread her legs, giving him all the access he could want.

With a sudden jerk of her hips, Dana became a caged tigress, savagely ripping at his denim shirt. "We're wearing too many clothes." She jumped off his lap, made short work of her robe and bra and reached for the zipper of his jeans.

"I agree," he gasped. Marc stood and let her finish lowering his zipper while he got rid of the shirt. He kicked out of the jeans and pulled her tightly against him, putting his soul into a searing kiss.

When their lips finally parted, she smiled dreamily up at him and let her fingers wander over his chest and down his stomach. The muscles in his belly clenched and it took everything he had to let her touch.

Though her moves and the look in her eyes sent jolting electric impulses to his every nerve ending, he managed to stand still and let her touch him boldly. The power of their passion was showing her the way to trust. To trust in him and in their love.

Tentatively, she lowered her hand and rubbed it over his erection. Then she stroked him, curling her palm around and sliding up and down.

"That's all I can take." He grabbed her wrist. "Next time…maybe."

She laughed throatily as he tumbled back on the bed with her. With his feet still planted on the floor, she pushed him flat on the bed. Then she straddled him, grinning madly all the while.

"Now I have you where I want you," she told him.

"This is right where I want you, too." He helped lift her hips, then she slowly lowered herself down on him. "Forever, my love." The pure pleasure of having her surround him left him breathless.

She closed her eyes and took him in deeper by arching her hips and leaning back. His world narrowed down to simple feelings—tight and hot. Being buried to the hilt inside her was causing him to lose his mind.

Leaning over him, low enough for her hair to tickle his chest, she began to rock. Gliding back and forth, he could feel her internal muscles as they began to clench around him.

Dana was everything he'd ever wanted or needed. He could never have dreamed up such good fortune.

His instincts took over as he drove himself into her. Higher and faster they climbed. And when she found her release, he let the explosions push him over the edge, too.

She collapsed down on his chest, weeping and moaning his name. But Marc wasn't finished with her yet.

When his breath evened out, he tightened his arms around her back and lifted them both to a sitting position. Still entwined together, he encouraged her to wrap her legs around his waist.

"Marc?"

"What is it, darling? You can't take the heat?"

"No. It's just…" She hissed in a breath as he flicked a finger over the tip of her breast.

"Say you'll marry me, my love." He was barely able to talk.

"I…" Her breathing was ragged, too, her heavy-lidded eyes were glazed and every breath seemed torn from her lungs.

"Say it, Dana. Say yes." He felt himself growing thick again as he trailed kisses down the side of her neck.

"Yes. I'll marry you. Oh, yes…" she screamed.

Finally. Thank the Lord.

With his tears threatening to spill over, Marc took his time and showed her how powerful their love could be.

He gave her everything he had. And he would always give her everything he was made of—as proof of his passion.

Epilogue

"You sure were a beautiful bride, Dana." Imogene Danforth Shakir hugged her cousin's new wife.

"Only thanks to you and Nicola, I can assure you." Dana shifted from one foot to the other, trying to relieve the pressure on her poor toes. "I really appreciate your help with the dress and everything else. I never would've gotten through this wedding without you."

Imogene, with her expensively cut blond hair and those dazzling green eyes, had done everything she could to turn Dana into a beautiful, if not blushing, bride.

The mid-morning sun filtered down on the wide front porch of Harold and Miranda Danforth's stunning home in the historical district of Savannah. The wedding had taken place a little over an hour ago in an elegant side garden of the old house. But Dana could hardly wait for the reception to be over so she and Marc could go home alone again.

"Where is your new husband?" Imogene asked.

Dana pointed to where Marc, with his jacket off and his shirtsleeves rolled up, was playing ball with another man and two small cousins under a huge magnolia tree. She knew security guards were stationed nearby and out of sight, but everyone would have to move inside soon. The cartel might still want revenge.

She put her hands on her hips. "He's really just a big kid at heart."

Imogene chuckled and waved a hand toward her cousin. "I need to give him my best wishes. I can't stay." She called to Marc then turned back to Dana. "He's always been good with kids. I've often thought he would end up making the best father of any of the Danforth men. Do you two plan on starting a family right away?"

"We're trying," Dana hedged breezily.

Marc swung up on the porch and stepped between the two women. He slipped an arm around each one.

Imogene leaned over and kissed his cheek. "Congratulations, Marc. You certainly picked a winner with Dana. She's one of the few women in the world who can hold her own with your father. Well, besides Nicola, of course."

"I did all right, huh?" Marc laughed, beaming over at his cousin.

Imogene rolled her eyes and changed the subject. "Was that your old buddy, Ben Hasgood, you were playing ball with? I didn't think you'd ever speak to him again after what he did last year. Why is he here?"

"I invited him," Marc admitted. "I owe Ben a lot for saving me from making a huge mistake with my life. If it weren't for him, I might've actually married the wrong woman. Instead, I found exactly the right woman."

He leaned over to Dana and tenderly kissed her lips. Then he drew his hand in a big arch, encompassing the virtual sea of relatives that had gathered on the lawn and in the various rooms of the big old mansion. "I'm glad so many family members could make it home for the wedding on such short notice."

A shadow moved across Imogene's face and Marc tightened his grip around her shoulders. "I know, Genie," he whispered, using her old childhood nickname. "I wish Victoria was here, too. She's the only one missing and it doesn't seem the same."

Dana remembered Marc's discussion about how his cousin, Victoria, had been missing for five years. Dana had never worked with the FBI's missing person's division, but she truly wished she could help find out what had happened. Perhaps a few well-placed calls would help.

It was Imogene's turn to shake her head. "It's been so long. Don't let it spoil your beautiful day." She leaned around Marc to talk to Dana. "Did I hear correctly that you've taken leave from the FBI? What do you plan to do?"

"First, Marc and I intend to help rid the Danforth family of the cartel and Ernesto Escalante once and for all. Then when the family is finally free, Marc wants me to help him head up the new Danforth Family Foundation."

Imogene smiled broadly. "I've heard about it. I know you two will make a difference in a lot of lives." She stepped away from them. "I'm sorry we have other plans and can't stay."

"We're just glad you and Raf could make it to the wedding," Marc told her. After a few seconds hesitation, he continued, "Actually, I'm just glad to be here myself." He said the words with a smile, but his expression was somber.

"I read in the paper that David Chastain disappeared after he was indicted for framing you," Imogene told him with a shake of her head. "Does that mean you're totally off the hook?"

"Even though Marc has been exonerated, the Danforths still have to watch out for the cartel," Dana put in. "At least until we get Escalante."

Dana and Marc bade goodbye to his cousin.

"Is dinner almost ready?" Marc asked as he returned his full attention to his bride.

"Why? Are you hungry?"

He nuzzled her temple and placed a soft kiss on her ear. "Uh-huh. But not for food."

She felt her nipples suddenly puckering against the satin material of her dress. And she found herself wishing again that they could go home to the farm right away.

"I've thought of a new *test,* and I'd like for us to give it a try, my love." Marc dragged her to his side and began running his hand up and down her spine, tantalizing her beyond belief.

Dana looked up into the eyes of the man she would love forever and sighed. "You've already made the grade, Dad."

"What?" He choked, blinked and stared into her eyes.

"I went to the doctor yesterday. This time, there's no doubt we're having a child." She kissed him and let all the pent-up love of a lifetime shine through it, telling him how she felt.

Love and trust were already creating the very best proof of their passion.

* * * * *

Watch for TERMS OF SURRENDER
by Shirley Rogers,
the next DYNASTIES: THE DANFORTHS,
coming in November from Silhouette Desire.

DYNASTIES: THE DANFORTHS

**A family of prominence...
tested by scandal, sustained by passion.**

TERMS OF SURRENDER

(Silhouette Desire #1615, available November 2004)

by **Shirley Rogers**

When Victoria and rebellious David Taylor
were forced into close quarters, former feuds turned
into fiery passion. But unbeknownst to all, Victoria was
no farmhand—she was the long-lost Danforth heiress!
Could such a discovery put an end to
their plantation paradise?

Available at your favorite retail outlet.

If you enjoyed what you just read,
then we've got an offer you can't resist!

Take 2 bestselling love stories FREE!

Plus get a FREE surprise gift!

Clip this page and mail it to Silhouette Reader Service™

IN U.S.A.
3010 Walden Ave.
P.O. Box 1867
Buffalo, N.Y. 14240-1867

IN CANADA
P.O. Box 609
Fort Erie, Ontario
L2A 5X3

YES! Please send me 2 free Silhouette Desire® novels and my free surprise gift. After receiving them, if I don't wish to receive anymore, I can return the shipping statement marked cancel. If I don't cancel, I will receive 6 brand-new novels every month, before they're available in stores! In the U.S.A., bill me at the bargain price of $3.80 plus 25¢ shipping and handling per book and applicable sales tax, if any*. In Canada, bill me at the bargain price of $4.47 plus 25¢ shipping and handling per book and applicable taxes**. That's the complete price and a savings of at least 10% off the cover prices—what a great deal! I understand that accepting the 2 free books and gift places me under no obligation ever to buy any books. I can always return a shipment and cancel at any time. Even if I never buy another book from Silhouette, the 2 free books and gift are mine to keep forever.

225 SDN DZ9F
326 SDN DZ9G

Name	(PLEASE PRINT)	
Address	Apt.#	
City	State/Prov.	Zip/Postal Code

Not valid to current Silhouette Desire® subscribers.

Want to try two free books from another series?
Call 1-800-873-8635 or visit www.morefreebooks.com.

* Terms and prices subject to change without notice. Sales tax applicable in N.Y.
** Canadian residents will be charged applicable provincial taxes and GST.
  All orders subject to approval. Offer limited to one per household.
  ® are registered trademarks owned and used by the trademark owner and or its licensee.

DES04R   ©2004 Harlequin Enterprises Limited

introduces an exciting new family saga with

DYNASTIES: THE DANFORTHS

A family of prominence...
tested by scandal, sustained by passion!

THE CINDERELLA SCANDAL by Barbara McCauley
(Silhouette Desire #1555, available January 2004)

MAN BENEATH THE UNIFORM by Maureen Child
(Silhouette Desire #1561, available February 2004)

SIN CITY WEDDING by Katherine Garbera
(Silhouette Desire #1567, available March 2004)

SCANDAL BETWEEN THE SHEETS by Brenda Jackson
(Silhouette Desire #1573, available April 2004)

THE BOSS MAN'S FORTUNE by Kathryn Jensen
(Silhouette Desire #1579, available May 2004)

CHALLENGED BY THE SHEIKH by Kristi Gold
(Silhouette Desire #1585, available June 2004)

COWBOY CRESCENDO by Cathleen Galitz
(Silhouette Desire #1591, available July 2004)

STEAMY SAVANNAH NIGHTS by Sheri WhiteFeather
(Silhouette Desire #1597, available August 2004)

THE ENEMY'S DAUGHTER by Anne Marie Winston
(Silhouette Desire #1603, available September 2004)

LAWS OF PASSION by Linda Conrad
(Silhouette Desire #1609, available October 2004)

TERMS OF SURRENDER by Shirley Rogers
(Silhouette Desire #1615, available November 2004)

SHOCKING THE SENATOR by Leanne Banks
(Silhouette Desire #1621, available December 2004)

Available at your favorite retail outlet.

COMING NEXT MONTH

#1615 TERMS OF SURRENDER—Shirley Rogers
Dynasties: The Danforths
When Victoria Danforth and rebellious David Taylor were forced into close quarters on the Taylor plantation, former feuds turned into fiery passion. But unbeknownst to all, Victoria was no farmhand—she was the long-lost Danforth heiress! Could such a discovery put an end to their plantation paradise?

#1616 SINS OF A TANNER—Peggy Moreland
The Tanners of Texas
Melissa Jacobs dreaded asking her ex-lover Whit Taylor for help, but when the smashingly sexy rancher came to her aid, hours spent at her home turned into hours of intimacy. Yet Melissa was hiding a *sinful* secret that could either tear them apart, or bring them together forever.

#1617 FOR SERVICES RENDERED—Anne Marie Winston
Mantalk
When former U.S. Navy SEAL Sam Deering started his own personal protection company, the beautiful Delilah Smith was his first hire. Business relations turned private when Sam offered to change her virgin status. Could the services he rendered turn into more than just a short-term deal?

#1618 SHEIKH'S CASTAWAY—Alexandra Sellers
Sons of the Desert
Princess Noor Ashkani called off her wedding with Sheikh Bari al Khalid when she discovered that his marriage motives did not include the hot passion she so desired. Then a plane crash landed them in the center of an island paradise, turning his faux proposal into unbridled yearning…but would their castaway conditions lead to everlasting love?

#1619 BETWEEN STRANGERS—Linda Conrad
Lance White-Eagle was on his way to propose to another woman when he came across Marcy Griffin stranded on the side of the road. Circumstances forced them together during a horrible blizzard, and white-hot attraction kept their temperatures high. Could what began as an encounter between strangers turn into something so much more?

#1620 PRINCIPLES AND PLEASURES—Margaret Allison
CEO Meredith Cartwright had to keep playboy Josh Adams away from her soon-to-be-married sister. And what better way to do so than to throw herself directly into his path…and his bed. But Josh had an agenda of his own—and a deep desire to teach Meredith a lesson in principles…and pleasures!

SDCNM1004